Praise for Arlene James

"Delightful characters make Arlene James'
story touching."
—*RT Book Reviews* on *Her Small-Town Hero*

"*His Small-Town Girl* is a warm, loving
and engaging story."
—*RT Book Reviews*

"Incredibly tender, solid
and very satisfying story."
—*RT Book Reviews* on *A Mommy in Mind*

"A warm, resounding story of love."
—*RT Book Reviews* on *A Love So Strong*

Praise for Kathryn Springer

"*Family Treasures* is extremely touching,
effective and satisfying."
—*RT Book Reviews*

"Kathryn Springer has a knack for character
development."
—*RT Book Reviews* on *For Her Son's Love*

"*By Her Side*, by Kathryn Springer,
is an excellent book."
—*RT Book Reviews*

"Springer's combination of humor,
family values and longing will reach out
from the pages and touch readers' hearts."
—*RT Book Reviews* on *Front Porch Princess*

ARLENE JAMES

says, "Camp meetings, mission work and church attendance permeate my Oklahoma childhood memories. It was a golden time, which sustains me yet. However, only as a young widowed mother did I truly begin growing in my personal relationship with the Lord. Through adversity, He has blessed me in countless ways, one of which is a second marriage so loving and romantic it still feels like courtship!"

The author of more than seventy novels, Arlene James now resides outside Dallas, Texas, with her beloved husband. Her need to write is greater than ever, a fact that frankly amazes her, as she's been at it since the eighth grade. She loves to hear from readers, and can be reached via her Web site at www.arlenejames.com.

KATHRYN SPRINGER

is a lifelong Wisconsin resident. Growing up in a "newspaper" family, she spent long hours as a child plunking out stories on her mother's typewriter and hasn't stopped writing since! She loves to write inspirational romance because it allows her to combine her faith in God with her love of a happy ending.

A Mother's Gift

Arlene James

Kathryn Springer

Steeple
Hill®

Published by Steeple Hill Books™

STEEPLE HILL BOOKS

Steeple
Hill®

Recycling programs
for this product may
not exist in your area.

ISBN-13: 978-0-373-87589-4

A MOTHER'S GIFT

Copyright © 2010 by Harlequin Books S.A.

The publisher acknowledges the copyright holders of the
individual works as follows:

DREAMING OF A FAMILY
Copyright © 2010 by Deborah Rather

THE MOMMY WISH
Copyright © 2010 by Kathryn Springer

www.SteepleHill.com

Printed in U.S.A.

CONTENTS

DREAMING OF A FAMILY

Arlene James

This one is for you, Ross, because you've made so many of this mom's dreams come true.

For God does speak—now one way, now another—
though man may not perceive it. In a dream,
in a vision of the night, when deep sleep falls
on men as they slumber in their beds…
—*Job* 33:14, 15

Prologue

They built the swing set beneath the magnificent old hickory tree that sheltered the backyard from the worst of the summer sun, the leaves rustling gently in the steady Oklahoma breeze. Dixie's parents came to help, delighted to provide their young grandson, Clark, with outdoor play equipment, now that he was old enough to begin to enjoy it.

The first dream came that very night, and it was always the same in the weeks thereafter.

Dixie woke, in her dream, and rose to calm sunshine and a sense of well-being. The next instant she stood at the sink in her homey kitchen, the smell of coffee in the air. Looking up, she saw at once through the window that the giant hickory had fallen, obliterating the newly erected swing set. A horrible feeling of panic seized her, for she knew, without reason or incentive, that Clark had somehow been on that swing set when the old tree had fallen.

At precisely that point, she always woke in reality.

Rushing down the hall, she would open the door and poke her head into Clark's quiet room to find him sleeping soundly in his low bed with the added railings, his dark hair curling against his pillow. The panic would ease. Sense would return.

No one had to tell her that her dream, and her fears, came

from the tragic death of her husband, Clark's father, Mark, over a year earlier.

Then, one night around the end of April, the dream inexplicably changed.

As always, Dixie woke, found herself in the kitchen, looked out the window over the sink, saw that the tree had fallen and *knew* that Clark had been on that swing set. This time, however, a man was there.

In her dream she thought to herself sadly, "That is not Mark."

This man stood tall and leanly muscled, his inky hair shorn high and tight in a military cut. She could not see his face, for he stood slightly turned away, not quite in profile, his head tilted to one side as if listening for something. All at once, he bent forward, his hands held out in front of him. He seemed to test the leaves, lightly moving his hands through them, then he calmly parted the branches of the fallen tree, and Clark, her own little son, leaped happily into the arms of this man who was *not* Mark.

Dixie woke with a start. Appalled, she recalled her mother's words of the day before.

"You can't grieve forever, Dix. Mark wouldn't have wanted that. It's time to start thinking about dating again. Open your heart to the idea of a new marriage, and God will bring the right man."

This, Dixie thought bitterly, would be the same God Who had callously taken the love of her life, her high-school sweetheart, the father of her son. How, she wondered, could she even think of marrying again when Mark would never know the joy of his son's third birthday? Never again would he see his son's smiling face or mark his growth against the doorjamb of his bedroom or feel his little arms about his neck.

Dixie blamed her mother's insensitive words for the change in her dream, just as in her heart of hearts she secretly blamed God for the freak accident that had taken her husband's life. Without quite realizing it, she blamed God for Mark's death almost as much as she blamed herself.

Chapter One

"You haven't been to church in over a year, Dixie," her father said, rubbing a thick hand over his coarse, closely cropped, steel-gray hair.

Dixie folded a bath towel and placed it atop the growing stack on her kitchen table. Small, round and battered, it had seen better days, as had the suite in the formal dining room.

"You don't have to remind me how long it's been since I buried my husband, Dad."

Sitting in a wobbly chair at that table, Samuel Wallace shook his head sadly. "I know I don't, sugar lump. It's just that I'm concerned about you laying out of church. With Mother's Day and your own mother's birthday falling on the same date this year, it seems like a good time to be in the Lord's house."

Dixie lowered her gaze as she reached for a small striped T-shirt from the laundry pile. "This is the third time we've had this conversation in the past two weeks."

"And we'll keep having it until you agree to join us in church," Sam insisted in his gravelly voice.

"I'm just not ready, Dad."

"It's her one wish, Dixie, to have her only child and grandchild in church with her on that special day. That's all she wants, Dix, just to have the family together in the pew again."

But the family wouldn't be together, Dixie thought, *not without Mark.*

Pulling another towel from the jumble, Dixie surreptitiously sucked in a deep breath before making the first fold. She did not wish to respond to her father in anger, but really, her mother was being terribly insensitive of late. Not only had Vonnie Wallace started urging Dixie to date and think about marrying again, now she asked this.

Her movements brisk and efficient, Dixie folded and stacked the towel. "I'm not sure I'll ever be able to sit in front of that altar again without seeing Mark's casket there."

"It was difficult for us the first few times, too, sugar lump," Sam rasped, his hazel eyes glimmering, "but you, Clark and the church are all the family we have. Mark would not have wanted us to pull back from any of that."

No, Mark would not have wanted that. No one valued family and connections more than Mark had. An orphan from the age of eleven, he'd grown up in a series of foster homes, so family had meant everything to him. That was one reason why it was so hard for her to go on without him, but her parents did not understand. In their world, loss and trauma were just experiences to be put behind.

She had tried to tell them, to explain about that day, but even if she'd been completely honest, they couldn't possibly understand. They had not been in the boat with Mark when it hit the pylon. They had not prayed frantically in the moments before, when it became clear that the structure was not a floating buoy. They had not screamed her husband's name upon impact or seen the bloody gash across his neck and shoulder as he hit the water. They had not begged God for Mark's life as blackness overwhelmed all else. They had not awakened in a hospital bed days later with broken bones and a head injury to be told that a best friend and husband of five years was dead and gone.

How could she sit in that church and not remember that awful day? How could she celebrate Mother's Day when Mark would never know another Father's Day with the son he had so desperately desired?

As if summoned by her thoughts, Clark ran into the room, *vroom*ing as he drove a plastic car in his little hand on a highway of air. At nearly three, Clark never walked anywhere, and he delighted in no one as he did Sam. "Pop-Pop!"

Sam Wallace caught Clark in his arms and lifted him onto his lap, pushing aside his coffee cup with the back of one hand to be sure that it was safely out of reach. "Hello, there, hot rod. How's my best boy? Been playing on that swing set out back?"

"Swing, swing, swing," Clark chanted, swaying side to side on his doting grandfather's lap.

Pushing away images of the dream, Dixie smiled even as she rolled her eyes. "All I ever hear is swing, swing, swing." She shook her head, her softly curling, golden-brown hair swishing just above her shoulders. "I'll be so glad when he's old enough to go in and out on his own."

"Ha! I'll remind you of that when he's driving you crazy by fanning the door every five minutes," Sam said, rising to his feet with Clark in his arms.

Still robust at sixty-four and recently retired from the diesel mechanics shop that he'd run for a full quarter century, one of Sam's first postretirement projects had been to erect the swing set beneath the old hickory in Dixie's backyard in time for warm spring weather. He and Clark headed out there now.

"Fifteen minutes, you two," Dixie instructed, glancing at the clock over the white enamel stove. "I have to get to the grocery store before I can make lunch."

"No problem. I've got the Old Codgers' Bible study in half an hour," Sam said with a wink. That was his affectionate name for the senior men's Thursday meeting, which ended with lunch at a local restaurant.

"And be careful," Dixie called, shivering a little.

"Don't worry," Sam told her, lingering a moment in the back door. "Just think about Mom's request. And while you're at it, Dix, you might want to remember what she went through to have you."

Dixie frowned as the door closed behind him. *Low blow,* she thought. Was it her fault that her mother had had to suffer through numerous miscarriages and several surgeries before finally carrying a child to term at the age of thirty-six?

"And one more thing," Sam said, opening the door again to stick his head back inside. "We owe Vonnie for skipping the big six-oh last year."

"I didn't ask anyone to curtail celebration of Mom's sixtieth birthday," Dixie pointed out softly.

"No one said you did. We all felt it was too soon after the tragedy. But that was fourteen months ago. It's time to move forward again, Dix."

Not fourteen months, Dixie thought, as he disappeared again. Merely thirteen months, two weeks and two days.

Clark had gotten lanky all of a sudden, Dixie realized, lifting him into the seat at the front of the grocery cart. His baby fat had gone to long legs and arms in a matter of weeks. She'd be buying him new pants again before she knew it. She couldn't help wondering how else he would take after his father. Would his dark, curly hair lighten and streak, as her own medium golden-brown tended to do in the summer sun, or would it stay as glossy as his father's dark chocolate-brown had done? Clark had her green eyes, rather than Mark's blue ones, but Clark's were lighter than her own dark green ones. Now suddenly he was showing signs of having inherited his father's long, lean frame rather than her short and, in her opinion, too-curvy one. If only Mark were here to see his son grow.

She turned the cart down the nearest aisle. A familiar salt-and-pepper head lifted from the perusal of a soup can.

"Dixie!" Bess Slade dropped the can into her shopping buggy and quickly pushed it down the aisle. "How good to see you."

Bess had been Vonnie Wallace's best friend since she and her son had joined the church some eleven or twelve years earlier, after Bess's divorce. At one time, much had been said about getting Dixie and Bess's son together, a plan Dixie had greatly resented, as she was already going steady with Mark. She'd even accused her parents of not approving of Mark, a charge they had adamantly denied. It was only, Vonnie had insisted, that Bess dreamed of a perfect marriage for her son, one similar to those of his older sisters, one far different from that which Bess herself had experienced.

Because Joel Slade was four or five years older than Dixie, their paths had not crossed, and Vonnie had made the whole matchmaking thing sound like Bess's idea. As a result, Dixie had avoided Bess as best she could over the years. Yet the woman had been nothing but kind and thoughtful in those awful days and weeks following Mark's death. Remembering how Bess had quietly slipped around her parents' house at the reception following Mark's funeral, keeping dishes washed and glasses filled, Dixie put on a smile.

"Hello, Bess. How are you?"

Bess delayed answering while she made a fuss over Clark, exclaiming what a handsome boy he was and how much he'd grown. Eventually, however, she came to a reply.

"I am so excited. Joel is finally home. After ten years, he's left the Marine Corps and decided to finish college here in Lawton."

"That's nice," Dixie replied blandly, but in the back of her mind she was hearing her mother say that it was time for her to start thinking of dating again. One surely had nothing to do with the other, though. Any idea of getting Dixie together with Joel Slade had surely evaporated long ago. Surely *not.*

"Yes, it is," Bess went on. "And speaking of nice, Joel and I both are very pleased about being invited to join your family for

Vonnie's birthday. That it's Mother's Day, as well, will make it even more of a celebration."

Dismayed, Dixie made a concerted effort not to gasp. "Will you excuse me, Bess?" she said, turning the cart about. "I just remembered something."

"Of course. I'm so glad I ran into you. Bye-bye, Clark. Such a handsome boy," she said for the second time, but Dixie was already mentally determining how she was going to nip this matchmaking nonsense in the bud.

By the time Dixie got Clark back into the car and drove through Lawton, then covered the five-plus miles to her parents' small acreage, she had put together a stern little speech. Clark on her hip, she stepped up onto the porch, and opened the door straight into the living room without bothering to knock. Her mother greeted her from the sofa, where she sat watching a television game show, her pale curly hair caught at the nape of her neck.

"Dixie. What a nice surprise." Pointing the remote, she shut off the TV and stood, reaching out for Clark, who went to her readily. "How's my darling today? Have you had lunch yet?"

"No, we haven't."

Vonnie turned and carried Clark through the swinging door at one end of the sofa, saying, "Come, let me fix you something. Dad's gone to his weekly Bible study."

"I know. He stopped by the house first."

"Did he?" Vonnie looked over her shoulder in surprise. "That's nice."

Silent on the subject, Dixie followed her mother into the kitchen.

Vonnie carried Clark to the high chair in the corner of the room near the trestle table, before moving to the refrigerator. While Dixie stewed and worked up her courage, Vonnie took out sandwich makings and carried them to the work island that was the heart of her warm brick-and-tile kitchen.

"Did Sam mention Mother's Day?" Vonnie asked innocently.

"You mean, did he pressure me to attend church with you that day? Yes, yes, he did."

Vonnie paused in the act of opening a jar of mayonnaise. "I'm sorry, Dixie," she finally said. "I never meant for you to feel pressured."

"But you did mean to invite Bess and Joel Slade to join us," Dixie accused petulantly.

Vonnie came around the island to lean against the counter. Dressed much as her daughter was, in jeans, a simple T-shirt and tennies without socks, her long, curly blond hair caught in a clasp at the nape of her neck, Vonnie looked decades younger than her nearly sixty-one years. Though a little plumper than Dixie, Vonnie could have passed for her sister, except for the silver in Vonnie's pale gold curls.

"And that's a problem because…"

Dixie shoved her hands into her hair, drawing it back from her face. The gesture emphasized the slight widow's peak from which her thick, wavy hair fell in a natural part. "Don't you think I know what you're up to, Mom? All this talk about me dating again, and now I find out you've invited the Slades to your celebration. You and Bess tried to push Joel Slade on me once before, or don't you remember?"

Vonnie didn't even try to deny it. "That was eons ago. You were a girl."

"And now I'm a widow."

Vonnie bowed her head, arms folded.

"Honestly, Mom," Dixie went on, "what am I supposed to think? First you say I should start dating again, and the next thing I know Joel Slade is in town and joining us for your celebration! Seems obvious to me."

Vonnie sighed. "You know, Dixie, we used to get on rather well, you and I."

"We still would if you'd stop trying to make me get over Mark's death!" Dixie snapped.

Without a word, Vonnie walked to the table, picked up Clark and carried him into the hallway and through the door of the playroom that she and Sam had outfitted for him. Dixie heard her murmuring to the boy before she came out again and closed the door behind her. To Dixie's shock, when Vonnie marched back into the kitchen, she came loaded for bear.

"Not everything is about you, Dixie!" Vonnie said heatedly. "It's *my* birthday! Mine! Is it so wrong to want my best friend at the table with me?"

"Your best friend *and* her son," Dixie pointed out.

Her mother's anger had set her back. Vonnie didn't get angry. Over the past year or so, unfortunately, Dixie's own temper had grown shorter and shorter. Today, however, the provocation surely justified the reaction. Didn't it?

"It's not just my birthday," Vonnie pointed out. "It's also Mother's Day, and Bess's son is finally home. What was I supposed to do, Dixie? Tell Bess to come along but leave Joel at home? Save her celebration for another time?"

It did sound unreasonable when put like that, but Dixie could not quite give up her pique. "If you'd limited the invitation to her, she would have declined. Problem solved."

Vonnie parked her hands at her ample hips. "It isn't a problem for anyone but you, Dixie! After all he's been through…" Vonnie paused and closed her eyes as if calming herself. "I happen to think very highly of Joel, and you would, too, if you'd ever met him."

"That's just the point, isn't it, Mother?" Dixie accused. "You want me to meet him because you want me to stop grieving my husband and start dating other men!"

"Is that a crime?" Vonnie asked, spreading her hands. "I just want what's best for you, Dixie. I always have."

"I'm not seventeen anymore," Dixie insisted. "I'm a twenty-six-year-old adult. I can decide for myself what's best for me."

"Dixie, you're a young, single mother with her whole life ahead of her," Vonnie pointed out pleadingly. "I don't want you to spend it alone. Mark wouldn't want you to spend it alone. That's all I'm saying."

Dixie turned aside thoughts of what Mark might have wanted. Being alone was what she deserved, but she could never say that to another living soul. Besides, that wasn't the point.

"And what about Clark? He needs a father," Vonnie said.

Dixie jumped on that with both feet. "Mark is Clark's father!"

"This isn't about Mark. It's about you and Clark." Vonnie thumped her fist against her breastbone. "You know that your father and I loved Mark Stevenson with our whole hearts, but Mark is gone. Don't use his death as an excuse to stop living. And don't think I'm going to let you use this nonsense about the Slades to get out of going to church on Mother's Day!"

Dixie blanched. She had been thinking that a refusal might be justified by her mother's manipulation, but Vonnie had cleanly swept that ground from beneath her feet. She scrambled for fresh purchase, her chin trembling. "You know what being there will do to me."

"You have to face it sometime, Dixie. Besides, you're the one who insisted that the service be at the church rather than the funeral home."

"Mark loved that church," Dixie whispered.

"He loved God more," Vonnie said. "When are you going to stop being angry at God, Dixie?" she asked. "When will you stop blaming Him for Mark's death?"

"I…I…" Dixie felt the hot tears start, but she shook her head. "You don't know what it was like. You don't know…." She bit her lip, hugging herself.

"You're right," Vonnie admitted. "I don't know what it's like to lose a husband, but I know that Mark would not want your anger or your continuing grief. And you know as well I do that he would not want Clark raised as an only child."

Dixie jerked as if she'd been slapped. Everyone knew that Mark had wanted "a dozen" children. She had, too, before that awful day, but without Mark… "Just because you couldn't be happy with one child," she accused thoughtlessly.

Vonnie gasped, but instead of reigniting her temper, Dixie's crass remark seemed to have saddened her mother.

"Oh, honey, no," Vonnie said, opening her arms and coming forward. "If I ever gave you that impression, please forgive me. You're all any mother could ever want."

Reduced in an instant to regretful tears, Dixie went straight into her mother's arms. "I'm sorry, Mom. I didn't mean that."

"You are the answers to my prayers, Dixie," Vonnie said, holding her close. "It breaks my heart, what you've been through. Your happiness means more to me than my own."

Dixie bit her lip, feeling small and selfish. "It's just so hard…without Mark," she whispered.

"I know, I know."

"Every day with Clark, I think of all that his father is missing, and it kills me."

"Dixie!" Vonnie scolded lightly, holding her daughter a little away so that she could cup her face in her hands. "Mark is in heaven. He's not missing a thing. But by holding yourself back, you are."

I should be, Dixie thought, but she shook her head. Her mother could not possibly understand. As for being angry at God, well, who wouldn't be?

"It just seems to me," she muttered in a shaky voice, "that the God of creation could control a little thing like a steering mechanism breaking in a speedboat."

"Absolutely He could," Vonnie agreed, leading her daughter to a chair at the table and sitting down next to her. "He could have prevented the martyrdom of the apostles, too, but for reasons we may not understand until we join Mark in heaven, God sometimes allows bad things to happen to His children. But He uses even those bad things for our good, Dixie, if we let Him. Even when those bad things are the results of our own actions, God can use them to bless us if we repent."

Stricken by that, Dixie suddenly knew what she had to do, but she merely nodded and smiled at her mother. "What about that lunch?" she asked, smiling shakily. "All at once I'm starving."

Vonnie cupped her daughter's cheek in one hand, concern written upon her face, but then she rose and cheerily set about building sandwiches while Dixie brought Clark back to the table.

When Sam came in more than an hour later, Dixie realized that she had lingered far longer than she'd planned.

"I still have to shop for groceries," she said, to her father's disappointment.

He walked her out to her car, carrying Clark, and buckled the boy into his safety seat before smiling down at her.

"So we're on for Mother's Day?"

Sighing inwardly, Dixie accepted the inevitable. "We'll be there on Mom's birthday."

Sam patted her and kissed the top of her head. "That's my little girl."

For a moment, she wished that were so. Oh, what she wouldn't give to go back and do it all again. This time she would not insist that she and Mark go out and test-drive that used boat. This time she would happily buy new, as he had wanted.

That night, after Dixie put Clark to bed, she got down on her knees and confessed her sin.

"Forgive me, Father. I've blamed You for what was my fault. Maybe I'll never know why You allowed that boat to careen out of control as it did, but I know that we were on it because I refused to buy a new one. I'm sorry for blaming You. I'm sorry for causing my husband's death. Help me to put aside my pain and worship You again."

The dream came with the storm that night. Spring being tornado season in Oklahoma, Dixie stayed up late to follow the weather report while Clark slept soundly in his room down the hall. She didn't sleep all that well since Mark had died, so she certainly didn't expect to drift off on the couch in the midst of a severe-weather alert, but drift off she did, curled up on the sofa in the den.

The next thing she knew, Dixie found herself standing at the kitchen sink. The morning felt like any other April day in Lawton, bright, a little windy with just a hint of the winter past mingling with the promise of summer to come. Looking up, she saw through the window that the enormous old hickory tree in the backyard had fallen on the swing set. Once more, the dark-haired man was there, this time with Clark safely snug in his arms. Stupendously handsome, his eyes dark and penetrating, he smiled at Dixie, and she felt a shock of recognition, though she knew she'd never seen him before. The man set Clark on his feet, and he was an older Clark, perhaps five or six years old. Hand in hand, they turned away from her, and in a blinding flash of insight, Dixie realized that the handsome stranger was taking her son away!

Panicked, she flew not to the door but to the window behind the round kitchen table in time to see the man let himself and Clark out the gate in the fence. Running from window to window inside, she followed their progress around the house and along the driveway to the sidewalk out front. As they headed off down the street, the man's hand upon Clark's shoulder, Dixie pounded on the window glass, raging for them to come back, but even she could not hear herself. Why, she wondered, in the illogical way of dreams, didn't the glass break so her voice could be heard?

Then suddenly they stopped, and the man bent to whisper into Clark's ear. Sobbing now, Dixie pressed her hands to the glass and stared at her son, his dark curls tousled by the breeze. The smile on the stranger's impossibly handsome face brightened, kicking up at one corner, as he snapped a jaunty salute. Abruptly, a sense of relief and well-being filled Dixie. Laughing, both the stranger and Clark waved before they turned and continued on their way.

"We'll be home soon, Mom."

Her son's words resounding in her mind, Dixie closed her

eyes, overcome with joy and gratitude. Wherever he was bound, her precious son was safe and well. There was nothing to fear.

Around her, the day came alive with the sounds of the city. Somewhere a cartoon played on a television set. The engine of a passing car hummed, its tires whirring. They would have to replace the swing set, she thought idly. Her father could help with that. Sam would be glad to erect another swing set for his beloved grandson.

Dixie woke gradually, feeling rested, the dream clear in her mind. How silly and nonsensical it seemed in the still light of early morning! She shivered, remembering the sharp, unformed fear and the sudden infusion of joy. Both faded as reality gradually intruded.

The television, she realized, still played softly, but the storm had passed without apparent harm. Dixie shut off the set, got up and went to dress in denim capris and a neat lime-green T-shirt. Because Clark always woke ravenous, she went to the kitchen to prepare breakfast, welcoming the chore as she welcomed anything that kept disturbing thoughts at bay. As she busied herself, the dream faded from her mind.

Until she looked out the window and saw that, in the previous night's storm, the old hickory had split and fallen, crushing the swing set beneath it.

Chapter Two

Stunned by the destruction of his swing set, Clark stood beside his mother in the backyard, enormous tears welling in his vibrant green eyes as he took in the fallen tree.

"It's all right, honey," Dixie told him. "Pop-Pop will build you another, and we can play in the park until it's ready."

"Park," he insisted solemnly, tugging at her hand with his own damp one.

But the storm had saturated the ground, and Dixie knew that mud holes would have swallowed the pea gravel in places. "Tomorrow," she promised, still shaken by what had happened.

The dream, of course, had nothing to do with the tree falling. That had been a result of the storm. Still, her skin prickled along her spine. They stayed in the house that day and busied themselves away from the kitchen window.

By midmorning of the next day, the first of May, the constant wind had dried the ground to a cushy firmness, so they set off on foot to walk two blocks to the playground, surrounded by a gravel jogging track. As soon as they turned onto the path toward the playground, they heard the clear voices of several children.

Dixie felt a pang of unexpected longing. More children of her own, she thought sadly, would have been a great blessing, but then she looked down at her eager son and smiled, thankful for the child she already had. Laughing lightly, she allowed herself to be tugged forward.

Well before they reached the play area, they drew near a bench where a man dressed in running gear sat in the dappled sunshine beneath a post oak tree. Tall and lean, with short black hair, he wore headphones as if listening to music. With his long legs stretched out before him and his head bowed, he seemed to be listening very intently.

Suddenly, Clark dropped Dixie's hand and veered toward the man, running full out. Before she could even register what was happening, Clark tripped over the man's feet and went sprawling, face-first, into the gravel. Stunned, Dixie froze, until Clark gasped and began to wail. Even as Dixie rushed forward, the man calmly leaned over, got his hands around Clark's little body and lifted the boy to his feet. By the time Dixie arrived, the trauma had given way to a gurgling giggle.

The man placed his big hand flat atop Clark's head and said, "Okay now?"

"I'm so sorry," Dixie said, skidding to a halt. "I don't know what happened, he just shot away from me."

"No harm done. You must be his mom," the man said, turning a smile up at her.

Gasping, Dixie stepped back, drawing Clark away from the stranger. It couldn't be! This was the face of the man in her dream.

Eyes of such a dark brown that they were almost black looked up at her from an all-too-familiar, impossibly handsome face. His smile cut grooved dimples into his flat cheeks, just as she recalled. Up close, his hair was blue-black. She shook her head, but if the man found that odd, he gave no indication. Telling herself that she was imagining things, Dixie stammered her thanks and rushed Clark away.

It couldn't be the same face, of course. Reason dictated that. Yet Dixie could not escape the notion that this was the man in her dream. Shaken, she glued herself to Clark's side, but the man, who sat at some distance, seemed to pay them no mind after that. Nevertheless, she cut the visit short and left the park by the side entrance, though it increased the walk home to three blocks.

By the time they reached her modest brick house with its offset garage, she had convinced herself that the man in the park only remotely resembled the man in her dream or that she had seen him somewhere else. Nevertheless, she called her father to come over and take a look at the fallen tree in order to determine what must be done to get up another swing in her yard. The fewer trips to the park—and the less chance of seeing the disturbing dark-haired man with the penetrating brown-black eyes—the better.

Two days passed before Dixie felt comfortable enough to venture out again. The tree, her father had told her, would have to be cut into pieces and moved out of the way before he could tell the extent of the damage to the swing set. Hopefully, only the crossbar would have to be replaced, but a proper length of pipe would need to be found, prepared and painted before repairs could be made. Clark, meanwhile, could not be denied his beloved swinging indefinitely, and so to the park they set off once more.

Chagrined to find the stranger, this time dressed in jeans and a simple beige T-shirt, sitting on the same bench, headphones in place, Dixie hoped to escape his notice. Clark, unfortunately, had other ideas. He began yelling, "Hello! Hello!" while they were still yards away. The man pushed back his headphones and smiled in their direction, removing any hope of avoiding an encounter. Clark tugged fiercely until Dixie released her hold on his hand.

With a sinking heart, she watched her young son race over to the man and crash eagerly into his knees. She heard the man's chuckle and saw how he placed his hand atop the boy's head.

"Why, it's my little friend from the other day. What's your name, son?"

Before Clark could answer, Dixie rushed over to take her child by the hand. "I'm sorry. A two-year-old thinks everyone he's encountered before is a friend."

"In this case, he's right," the man said, smiling. "But two?" He placed his hand atop Clark's head again. "He's much too tall for two."

"Almost three," Dixie amended. "Three in early July."

"Still, even for a three-year-old, he's a tall one."

"Swing," Clark said. "My swing broke."

"That's too bad. A boy needs his own swing."

The man gave Clark his full attention, and Dixie watched with dismay as her little boy honed in on that, like a sunflower that lifts its head to the noon sunlight. Perhaps her mother was right and Clark did need a fatherly influence beyond that of his grandpa. Was that what God was trying to tell her with her dream?

It could not be anything else. Still, this man's resemblance to the fellow in her dream was a figment of her imagination, nothing more. She was quite sure of it. In fact, she refused to believe that the dream contained any message at all. And yet, as she hurried him away, her son looked back at that stranger on the bench with undisguised longing.

Certain programs and organizations provided wholesome male influence for children, didn't they? Dixie made a mental note to check out what might be available in the Lawton area. Mark would not want their son to suffer for lack of male attention and guidance any more than she did.

Then again, Mark would want to be the one to give him everything that he needed.

Oh, Mark, she thought, *I'm so sorry.*

Her parents were waiting in the foyer when Dixie led Clark, in his new Sunday best, through the door of the church where she had grown up, found Christ, been baptized, married and buried her husband.

"How handsome!" Vonnie exclaimed, dashing tears from her eyes as she stooped to embrace her grandson.

"Thank you, sugar lump," Sam whispered, wrapping his arms around Dixie for a quick hug.

Vonnie straightened Clark's clip-on bow tie and brushed the buttons of his checked shirt with an adoring hand before Sam swept the boy up, posing with him so Vonnie could compare their navy-blue bow ties. Sam's had a stripe of red running through it. A collection of crazy bow ties was Sam's claim to fame, so of course Dixie had chosen a sedate version of the same for her son. Vonnie was still gushing over them when the outer door opened behind Dixie.

Vonnie turned, exclaiming, "Bess! And Joel. My, how wonderful you look." She moved forward for hugs. Dixie turned to encounter the top of a dark head of short, inky-black hair. Even before he moved back from the embrace and lifted his face, Dixie felt her skin prickle with gooseflesh.

"You!" she gasped. "You're Joel Slade!"

"Dixie? It was you in the park!" he exclaimed, his smile as wide as his face. He put out his hands, patting the air as if hunting for the boy. "And my little buddy," he said. "That would be Clark, yes? How wild is that?"

To Dixie's horror, two things happened at once. Clark launched himself at Joel Slade, his "friend" from the park, and she realized what had escaped her before—Joel Slade was not only the man in the park and, arguably, the man in her dream: Joel Slade was also blind.

Joel laughed, hugging the warm little body tight. So this was Clark. Clark!

"You've already met," Vonnie Wallace said.

"Imagine that!" his mother chimed in, excitement in her voice.

Despite his sternest warnings to himself, Joel couldn't help sharing her excitement just a little. To think that it had been Dixie Wallace and Clark in the park! It seemed unbelievable.

Correction, not Dixie Wallace. It was Dixie Stevenson now. Why had he never learned to think of her by her married name? Maybe because he'd last seen her in person almost a decade ago. He smiled, picturing her at seventeen.

She'd been a fresh beauty back then, with her long hair hanging down her back in a rich, rumpled swath of browns, golds and bronzes, her gently arched brows slightly darker. The widow's peak at the top of her forehead had emphasized the heart shape of her face, with its narrow chin, plump lips and large, dark eyes. He hadn't been able to tell their color from across the parking lot, but he knew from her school photos that they were an unusual shade of spruce-green. She had been pretty enough back then to make him wonder if he was doing the right thing by joining the Marine Corps. Had it not been for the tall, slender fellow on whose arm she had hung, Joel might even have tried to attract her interest back then, as his mother had always urged him.

Joel's senses had told him several things even as he'd accepted the boy's weight. For one thing, the boy hadn't come from the direction of his mother's voice. For another, a fond, familiar odor, like clean leather and fresh motor oil, had touched Joel's nostrils. He'd noticed it the first time they'd met since his return home. Joel smiled again, shifting the boy so he could put out his right hand.

"Sam? Is that you?"

The older man's burly mitt grasped Joel's. Stiff and dry, calloused from years of toil, it conveyed a genuine welcome, as had Vonnie's hug.

"How you doing there, Joel? Glad you could make it."

Joel turned his head slightly to dampen the sounds of people passing through and gathering in the foyer: footsteps, voices, sniffles here and there, gusting breaths, the rustle of fabrics. "It's good to be back, Sam. I've missed this church." He caught the sound of gulping and trembling breaths nearby. Dixie? Almost certainly.

He knew then that he had shocked her with more than just his identity. She hadn't realized that he was blind. He'd wondered about it that second time in the park. Given the way she'd reacted at their first meeting—the stunned silences, the gasping and gulping, the swiftness of her subsequent movements—he'd thought that she'd realized that he'd lost his sight and was repelled by it. After the second meeting, though, he'd wondered. Something about her reaction at that time had made him think that she had missed the signs. If he had known who she was, he would have told her, but even after two years he wasn't comfortable baldly announcing his blindness to every stranger, not that she'd given him much opportunity for that.

The boy's arms tightened about Joel's neck, and he felt that little head lower to his shoulder. At the same time, he felt her move closer. He was sure it was Dixie. He recognized the floral smell of her shampoo and wondered how long her hair was. She had worn it very long as a girl, but it had barely touched her shoulders in the last photo he'd seen. Was it the same length or had she cut it even shorter, as so many busy moms seemed to do?

Shutting off that line of thought, he concentrated on the boy. That warm little body cradled against his chest made gladness rise inside of Joel. The worst part of blindness for him was the isolation. He had never been so aware of his own skin as he was once he could no longer see beyond it. He literally craved touch now.

Patting the boy's back, he said, "How are you, buddy? Been to the park lately?" A nod against his shoulder. Joel winked in the general direction of Sam. How many times since he'd been back had Sam proudly told him that his grandson had been named after him? "I think it's time for an actual introduction." He found the boy's right hand with his and gave it a shake. "You are Clark Samuel Stevenson, and I am Joel Andrew Slade." A piano began to play. Joel instantly shut it out. "You can call me—" The boy was plucked abruptly from his grasp. "Joel," he finished.

At the same time, Dixie said, "Mr. Slade doesn't need to stand around holding you, Clark. Besides, it's time to go in."

Mr. Slade. Joel felt a flash of angry disappointment, even though he'd assumed that his blindness would repel her, which was one reason he'd foolishly asked his mother to keep it from her. He'd first told himself that it was because he was nothing to her and then because a mourning woman didn't need to know of anyone else's concerns. The truth was that he hadn't wanted any strikes against him before he even showed up in person.

Why it should matter, he didn't know. It was just that he couldn't get that face out of his memory, those two faces, one of them glowing with happiness, the other tiny, wrinkled and newborn. Some days he wished he'd never seen that photo of the two of them in that hospital bed.

His mother's arm slipped through his, giving it a supportive, encouraging squeeze. He returned it, plastering a smile on his face. Assuming that they were all about to move into the sanctuary, he stepped forward, only to feel a variety of warm presences. Sam. Dixie. Now Vonnie. Where, he wondered, was Clark? Murmurs and whispers told him that Dixie's parents had flanked her, one on either side.

"Ready?" Vonnie.

"Just think about today." Sam.

"We're right here."

They moved off, and Bess urged Joel to follow.

"A time for worship and celebration." Sam again.

"Take my hand." Vonnie.

"Gotta happen sooner or later, sugar lump."

"Clark." This from Dixie. "Remember what I told you. Best behavior."

"Okay, Mommy." Joel pinpointed the voice. Clark was walking along in front of his mother.

Joel heard people greeting Dixie and her parents. It became clear that Dixie had not been around the church in some time. She'd been part of the youth group when this had last been his regular church home, which meant that they had attended separate services, not that he had been all that faithful. After high school, he'd floundered a bit, halfheartedly attending junior college with no real idea of what he wanted to do with his life before settling on the Marine Corps.

Someone thrust a paper into his hand. A man called Bess by name.

"My son, Joel." She gave his hand a furtive tap, and he lifted it, felt it grasped, shaken. "Son, this is Emmitt Lively."

"How do you do?"

"Good to meet you."

They entered the larger room. Joel felt a moment of uncertainty as he sought to get his bearings. A guitar had joined the piano, but the sound seemed to be coming from different directions. Then he realized that the guitar was miked. Voices, movement and smells swamped him from every side. His mother smoothly steered his progress until they came to a halt. She reached out, making sure that his hand fell upon the end of a pew at the same time hers did. Then she gave him a little nudge on the hip. Another touch showed him the area through which he would need to move. Turning, he edged his way into the pew and kept moving until he sensed another body.

He felt behind him and sat, hearing a little voice say, "Joe?"

"Shh."

"Joe?"

He leaned forward, bumping shoulders with Sam, who said, "Come here, pal."

"Make him keep still," Dixie muttered.

There was a tussle, and a little shoe knocked against Joel's knee.

"Joe?" Clark said again. Joel smiled in the boy's direction, against a background of hushing sounds, and then a man's voice welcomed them to the service. After a few remarks, he asked everyone to stand for the opening hymn. Music swelled, live music from the sound of it, many more instruments than the old organ and piano that he remembered. Joel started to rise and found himself nearly knocked back down by a small body.

"Whoa," Sam said. Joel chuckled, gathering the boy into his arms once more. Dixie hissed from the other side of her father, but Sam just put his head next to Joel's and muttered, "Looks like you two are already old buddies." Joel nodded, smiling, as the congregation began to sing. "What?" Sam said, apparently talking to Dixie. "He's fine. Kids always go for the new face in the group."

Clark touched Joel's mouth then, as if asking why he wasn't singing. "Not a song I know," he explained softly.

Next to him, his mother's smoky alto lifted in praise. It was a beautiful sound to Joel, all those voices and instruments, with his mother's voice next to him. He pressed a hand between Clark's delicate shoulder blades and inhaled deeply, every cell aware that he stood in the house of God. A sense of peace, of true homecoming, crept over him, followed by the gentle elation of gratitude.

I am still a man, he thought, feeling that small body pressed to his, *and God is still God.* No disappointment and no challenge could overcome those two facts.

Dixie maneuvered past her father as the song ended and everyone once more took their seats for announcements. Sam grumbled, but he slid over when she motioned.

Ignoring her, Clark found something interesting about Joel's ear but then quickly moved on to his jaw, muttering, "Pop-Pop's jaw picky," as he patted Joel's chin.

Joel chuckled, and with a deep breath Dixie fought down a rising sense of irrational indignation. Sam's jaws were bristly and prickly even when freshly shaved, so it was no wonder that Clark was fascinated by Joel's smooth face, though given the blue-gray shadow beneath Joel's skin, Dixie couldn't imagine that he would stay freshly shaved for long.

Mark's beard had glistened rusty-brown, she remembered with a shock. How long had it been since she'd even thought of that? She glanced at the altar, a plain, heavy, oblong table of pale wood, and the vacant space before it. She closed her eyes, expecting horrific images of that day. When they did not materialize, guilt and resentment assailed her. She immediately pulled Clark into her lap.

Joel Slade frowned, and Clark looked at her curiously, his slender brows drawn together tightly.

"Be still," she whispered. He babbled something she couldn't quite discern. Ignoring it, Dixie fixed her gaze straight ahead, prepared for grief and sadness.

Not thirty seconds later, Clark attempted to crawl over into Joel's lap again. Caging him with her arms, she kept him with her, but then the congregation was called to the opening prayer. Standing with Clark in her arms, Dixie bowed her head and tried to concentrate on the poetic words of the pastor, but Clark squirmed and soon became heavy. She dipped slightly, intending to stand him on the pew, but the scamp wiggled away, and when she looked up, he was once more in Joel Slade's arms. This time he played with the Windsor knot in Joel's blue silk tie.

The combination of sky-blue silk against a slightly paler shirt was stunning with Joel's blue-black hair and black suit. Dixie wondered if Bess had chosen them for him, and just the fact that she wondered about something so personal irritated and perturbed her.

When they sat down again after the prayer, she pulled Clark back onto her lap and tried to occupy him by taking out an envelope and letting him draw on it with a pen. He kept leaning over to show it to Joel, who had no idea what was going on. Embarrassed, she tried to pass Clark to Sam, but Clark put up a noisy fight, which she had to curtail by giving up and placing a hand lightly over his mouth. That was when Joel Slade reached over and literally commandeered her son.

Dixie's mouth fell open at his high-handedness, and because he couldn't see her glower, she closed it with an audible snap. She spent the rest of the entire first half of the service fulminating, especially as Clark sat quietly on Joel's lap, his back to Joel's chest. Anytime he became restless, Joel whispered something into his ear, and Clark instantly quieted. Dixie could not control her resentment, telling herself that it wasn't fair.

That should be Mark, she thought. *That should be Mark.*

When the preaching started, Clark became restive again. She produced the paper and pen as inducement, but once Clark had them, he moved right back onto Joel's lap. Not content to simply scribble by himself, at one point, Clark offered the pen to Joel, poking him in the chin.

Mortified, Dixie hauled him onto her lap, cupped a hand over his ear and whispered, "Stop it, Clark. Joel can't see what you're doing. He can't see at all." In an effort to help him understand, she placed her hand over his eyes. "Joel can't see."

Joel frowned at Dixie, and none of it meant a thing to Clark, anyway. He shrugged off her hands and slid to the floor, banging up against Joel's knees. By that time, Joel had produced a small metal object about the size of a credit card. Taking a hardback hymnal from the pew pocket, he placed it on his lap. Then he found the open envelope on the pew next to him and flattened it atop the book, running his fingertips over it until he somehow located a clean spot. He placed the metal card on the paper, and Dixie saw that a small rectangle had been cut out of the center of the card, with tiny notches marking the long edges, top and bottom. A whisper in Clark's ear got Joel the pen. He then very carefully, using both hands, wrote Clark's name inside the rectangle.

Clark reclaimed the pen and spent the next twenty minutes leaning against Joel's knees while he scribbled inside the tiny rectangle, moving it every time he'd filled the spot. The paper was practically black by the time they rose for the closing hymn.

Dixie plucked the pen from Clark's grasp, but before she could pull him into her arms, Joel had set aside the book and paper and taken him up. Fascinated by the fact that Joel actually sang this time, the hymn apparently being familiar to him, Clark stared into the man's face. After a moment he reached up and touched Joel's eye with his finger. Joel flinched, but then he smiled and actually bowed his head for Clark's exploration.

"They're there," Dixie heard him whisper to the boy. "They just don't work anymore."

Dixie gulped, pity and embarrassment mingling with her feelings of resentment. She hated that Joel was blind, but she also very much disliked the fact that he had so entranced her son, against her wishes, and that she couldn't even call him on it! How, after all, did she challenge a blind man? The most she could do was take back her son as soon as the service ended.

"Come on, Clark. We don't want to burden Mr. Slade. Time to go to Nana's birthday dinner."

Joel Slade's mouth tightened as he released the boy, but he smiled and said, "Yeah, I'm looking forward to that myself." Even as his mother laid a hand on his forearm, though, he bent his head and spoke softly to Dixie, his breath stirring the hair over her ear. "And you don't have to worry about burdening me. I'm blind, not weak. Or stupid."

With that, he yielded to his mother's silent entreaty and followed her out of the pew, leaving Dixie with her face burning while her son followed him with hungry, worshipful, heartbreaking eyes. She was halfway up the aisle before she realized that she had hardly thought of Mark's funeral at all.

Chapter Three

"Look at this," Sam said, handing a long-stemmed pink rose to each of the women. "In honor of Mother's Day. Now, this is a classy restaurant."

Dixie made herself accept the flower. Sam was a man's man, a little rough and rugged, who wouldn't know class if it smacked him in the face with those roses, but he loved her mother, her and Clark with every fiber of his being. He could never understand why she'd like to dash that rose to the floor and stomp it, especially as she adored everything about being a mother. Still, she could not forget that, were it not for her, Mark would be here now enjoying this time in their son's life.

"No, no, Clark." The sound of her son's name spoken in Joel Slade's voice jarred Dixie. She whirled around to find Clark standing with his hands pressed flat against a large fish tank set into the rock wall of the restaurant's waiting area. Joel crouched beside him, speaking softly. "Tapping on a fish tank isn't good for the fish."

"He was just patting it," Dixie defended, rushing over to take her son by the hand.

Joel pushed up to his full height. Somehow, he seemed more imposing sightless than he might have otherwise. "If I could hear it from across the way," he said, nodding to the bench where their mothers now sat chatting, "then it must have been deafening to the fish on the other side of that glass."

Dixie lifted her chin. "I imagine your hearing is more acute than normal. At least, that's what I understand happens with—" She bit her lip, her flimsy outrage waning in the heat of her embarrassment.

"Blind people," he finished for her. "You can say it, you know."

Uncomfortable, Dixie cast a glance at her father's back. He rocked on his heels in front of Vonnie and Bess in the increasingly crowded waiting area. She edged closer to Joel, Clark's hand in hers to prevent him from tapping on the fish tank again. She knew that she had overreacted. "I—I'm sorry. I didn't mean to—"

"You're right, by the way," he interrupted cheerfully. "The loss of one sense does sharpen others. You begin to figure it out as soon as the initial panic is over. You start to realize how much sensory information you blocked out before."

Dixie smiled, realizing that he had intentionally derailed her apology. "It must have been terribly confusing at first."

"Yes, disorienting. Right after the explosion, I couldn't tell where I was, who was with me, what was happening. It was almost sensory overload, but all that seemed to matter was that I couldn't see. I had to get past that, accept it, before I could learn to decipher what my ears, nose and skin cells were telling me."

"It was an explosion, then?" Dixie prodded gently.

Joel nodded as casually as if they were discussing the weather. "IED on the side of the road in Iraq. The driver lost his leg, and the others took some shrapnel, but we were blessed not to lose lives."

"Blessed," Dixie parroted. "How can you say that?"

Joel shrugged. With his hands clasped behind his back and his legs spread, he looked every inch the Marine. "Soldiers deployed into war are putting their lives on the line every day. You learn to approach each moment as if that is the moment you'll be called upon to make the ultimate sacrifice. I could have lost my life that day, as have so many others. Instead, all that was required of me was my eyesight. Doesn't seem such a terrible thing by comparison."

Dixie cleared her throat, suddenly moved, and asked in a soft voice, "Didn't you ever ask, 'Why me?'" She had. From time to time over the past fourteen months, in one way or another, she had railed at God, demanding to know why her husband had to die. "It's just so unfair," she whispered.

"Why not me?" Joel asked. "Might as well be me as anyone else. I look at it this way. If Christ, Who was unfairly crucified, could go to the cross without complaint, how can I stay angry about this?"

"But if Christ had not gone willingly to the cross, He wouldn't have been the perfect, redemptive sacrifice," Dixie pointed out.

"If I hadn't gone willingly into the military, I wouldn't have been on that road in Iraq. Jesus didn't regret His sacrifice in the service of humanity. I can't regret my sacrifice in the service of my country. Not that the two equate in value," he quickly qualified, "or that I'm happy about losing my sight or that I didn't have some selfish reasons for joining up."

"Such as?"

"Pride. Career. College tuition."

"You have every reason to be proud," she said. "I'm sorry about your career."

Joel grinned and lifted a hand to the small of her back just as the hostess appeared. "There's still that college tuition."

"Wallace, party of six."

Dixie bowed her head and clutched her son's hand, feeling small and selfish for her own lingering anger at Mark's death. Obviously, God was showing her that she was not the only one to have suffered loss, and that her attitude about it still needed some adjustment.

After following her parents and Bess through the busy restaurant, Dixie took a seat across the table from Joel, with Clark in his booster seat at the end, more or less between them. While

Dixie kept Clark busy and glanced over her own menu, Bess quietly read from hers to Joel. Eventually, drinks were brought and choices were made. In the conversation that followed, they touched upon several topics. Then Vonnie asked Joel about his future plans.

Dixie was surprised to learn that he intended to practice law, and that he was far closer to attending law school than she could have imagined. He had been taking classes by computer for eighteen months and was, in fact, still doing so. During the upcoming summer semester at the local university, he would take the LSAT, but thanks to his military service and the efforts of an influential former commanding officer, he was already guaranteed a spot at the law school of his choice, provided his LSAT scores weren't an embarrassment and he kept his final grades up.

They talked about that until the meal came. They all bowed their heads while Sam spoke a blessing over the food. Dixie added her own quick, silent prayer.

Okay, Lord. I get it. Thank You. I understand now, and it will be different. I've been wallowing around in self-pity here for more than a year while others were facing their losses with courage and faith. I guess it took Joel Slade to show me that.

Surely that was the reason for her dreams and their encounters in the park and today. That and only that.

She lifted her head and looked straight into Joel's sightless eyes. The eerie feeling that he knew what she was thinking crept over her. She shook her head at her own foolishness at the same time as she shook out her napkin.

Clark dined off her plate and the table bread, but he routinely engaged Joel throughout the meal and vice versa. The two made a game of shifting around the saltshaker, and Dixie was amazed by how accurately Joel could track it. Sam had arranged for birthday cake to be served, much to Clark's delight, and Joel even seemed to relish Clark's enjoyment of his dessert.

"Man, he really loves chocolate, doesn't he?"

"Does he ever!" Sam confirmed, using his finger to swipe up the last vestige of chocolate frosting from his own plate. "Can't imagine where he got that." Everyone laughed when Sam popped his finger into his mouth.

The waiter soon returned with the check, and Joel instantly began digging out his wallet.

"I insist on paying for Mom's lunch," he announced. "My Mother's Day gift for her. And Dixie's," he went on, turning his face in her direction, "because Clark isn't old enough yet to honor her in that way."

A hot thrill shot through Dixie, a mixture of longing fulfilled and longing forever denied. The very fact that it had visited both shocked and alarmed her.

"No!" she blurted, bringing every eye at the table to her. How ironic that the sightless eyes were the ones to slice her composure to shreds. "I—I mean…this is Mom's day."

"It is," Joel agreed quietly, leaning forward slightly, "but there are two other mothers at this table."

To her horror, Dixie felt the burn of tears. Suddenly angry, she pushed back her chair, muttering, "I don't want to celebrate this day for myself."

"Dixie," Vonnie pleaded.

"I can't!" Dixie exclaimed. "Not when Mark will never celebrate another Father's Day." She shot to her feet. "I believe I'll visit the ladies' room. Excuse me, please."

She never noticed the rose that fell from her lap to the floor. Why would she, when she didn't want it? Then again, she didn't want to like Joel Slade, either, and she didn't.

She wouldn't.

"Joe!"

Joel smiled, shifting on the slatted bench. Finally, his persistence had paid off.

He'd sat in the warm sunshine, enjoying the mild spring weather and listening to a lecture on tape, for what felt like hours. The lecture, in fact, had long since ended, but Joel hadn't been able to make himself leave. He didn't know why, really. He had no reason to think that Dixie would welcome another encounter with him.

Dinner had ended awkwardly on Sunday, to say the least. After he'd offered to buy her meal, Dixie had avoided him like the plague, and he had no expectation of things being different now just because a couple days had passed. Yet, he'd come to the park on Monday and Tuesday and again today, lingering longer each time.

Even as he told himself that it was useless to remain, he heard the scruff of gravel and an agitated whisper that made his breath seize. Dixie. He knew it. Would she ignore him? She wouldn't have dared if he was sighted, but some people considered his blindness permission to simply pretend that he didn't exist. The sound of running feet had him sitting forward in anticipation.

"Clark?"

"Joe!"

He almost didn't get his arms out in time to catch the boy, as Clark seemed to launch himself from a dead run. Joel laughed in sheer delight, feeling those little arms slide about his neck.

"Hey, little buddy! How are you?" Shifting the boy to a sitting position on his lap, Joel rubbed Clark's head, loving the feel of all those springy curls.

"Joe," Clark burbled, "the tree still on my swing."

"It is? How did that happen?"

"The storm did it so it come down, and it's on my swing. Pop-Pop has to fix it."

"Is that right? Well, I'm sure your Pop-Pop can take care of it."

"Yeah," Clark said confidently. "Want to swing?"

Joel grinned. "I'd love to, but I'm not sure these swings are big enough for me."

Dixie spoke up then. "He can't swing, Joel, because he can't see. Remember? You go on and play now. I'll be over in a minute. Just stay in sight."

Joel helped Clark get down off his lap. "Later, pal."

"'Kay, Joe."

He listened to the boy run off toward the playground, which was quite close by, as Joel had chosen a bench on its perimeter. Tamping down his anger, he raised his face and asked calmly, "How've you been?"

She answered him with an abrupt question of her own. "Should you be out here by yourself?"

Joel set his back teeth. So that was how it was going to be. First, he couldn't swing because he couldn't see. Now this. "I don't need a keeper, thank you very much."

"How did you get here, anyway? Surely your mother didn't just drop you off."

"My mother is at her part-time job. I get around on my own, just as you do."

"But it's not like you can drive a car."

"I don't have to drive. There are excellent aids to help me navigate. I walked here from Mom's today with nothing more than a folding cane." He pulled it from his pocket to show it to her. "Which I didn't have to use, by the way."

"Why do you come here?" she asked, ignoring his explanation. "Can't you sit in the sun at home?"

Joel struck a nonchalant pose, one elbow balanced on the edge of the bench back. "I come here several times a week to run," he told her, "and, yes, sometimes just to sit in the sun and listen to my lectures. Do you have a problem with that, Dixie?"

"To run?" she echoed uncertainly, ignoring everything else.

"Yeah, you know, like those two people on that jogging trail over there."

A pause followed, during which he suspected she was checking out the jogging trail.

"How do you know there are two runners?"

"I heard two distinct strides when they ran by here a few minutes ago."

"Hmph. How do I know someone didn't tell you there were two?"

His jaw dropped. Why, he wondered, was she being so insulting? Maybe she thought it would offend him so badly that he would start avoiding her. Or maybe she just needed to convince herself that he wasn't a whole man. That smarted. More than it should have.

"Maybe you think I wear this gear by accident?" he snapped sarcastically, waving a hand to indicate his tracksuit and running shoes. "You probably think I can't even dress myself."

"Well, if you're going to be disagreeable…"

"If *I'm* going to be disagreeable?" But he already knew that he was talking to air. He could hear her footsteps carrying her away.

He sat where he was, wounded and angry, for several minutes. Then he got up and left the park. He felt the pavement of the sidewalk beneath his feet before he remembered to count his steps. Fortunately, he was familiar enough with the area by now that it was just a matter of locating the curb with his cane and turning in the right direction for home. Dealing with Dixie after this was going to take a good deal more thought, but deal he would. And so would she.

For the second time in Dixie's memory, prayer did not diminish her guilt. Sadly, nothing could change the fact that she was responsible for her husband's death, but she had expected to feel a little better, at least, about how she'd dealt with Joel Slade in the park. Unfortunately, such was not the case. Prayer only seemed to deepen her regret.

Driving toward her parents' place that Friday, Dixie admitted to herself that she still didn't know why she'd treated Joel as if he were a delusional invalid that day. She was not by nature a cruel person; yet, she had intentionally attacked Joel's pride. She'd seen him sitting there, looking whole and handsome and entirely capable, and she'd panicked. That was the only way she could describe what she'd felt: panic.

At the time, she had tried to justify her actions by telling herself that he'd been entirely open and nonchalant about his blindness the last time they'd talked. So why shouldn't she say what she was thinking, right? Except, she'd known in some perverse part of herself what she was doing. She just didn't really know why. True, she had hoped not to run into Joel again, but that did not really explain her reaction to seeing Joel there that day.

She was so disturbed by her own behavior that she hadn't been back to the park since and, after dropping off Clark at a popular Mothers' Day Out program, was now headed over to speak to her father about removing the tree from her backyard and rebuilding the swing set. Then she wouldn't have to worry about bumping into Joel Slade again.

At least something good had come of all her prayers since that day, Dixie told herself. In the midst of confessing her sin, she had suddenly recalled a Scripture read at Mark's funeral, Hebrews 12:22–24.

"But you have come to Mount Zion, to the heavenly Jerusalem, the city of the living God. You have come to thousands upon thousands of angels in joyful assembly, to the church of the firstborn, whose names are written in heaven. You have come to God, the judge of all men, to the spirits of righteous men made perfect, to Jesus, the mediator of a new covenant, and to the sprinkled blood that speaks a better word than the blood of Abel."

On the day of the funeral, all those words had meant to her was that her husband was no longer with her and their son. Now she finally, completely understood that he was not just apart from her; he was physically with Jesus, in the joyful company of countless angels, in the very presence of almighty God. Moreover, after thinking about that Scripture in the context of the other verses, she understood that prayer took her spirit to the very same place, a place where she, too, would one day physically dwell. She found that profoundly comforting, despite the guilt that tormented her.

Pushing aside thoughts of Mark and Joel Slade, Dixie parked the car behind her dad's diesel pickup truck and got out. It was a glorious day of crystalline sunshine and warm, soft air, the perfect day to be outside, so she wasn't surprised to find the house empty. She walked on through to the patio door, which stood ajar, and stepped out onto the flagstones, seeing her mother at once. Vonnie stood behind one of the chaise longues arranged around a glass-topped table in the center of the space. She was balancing a serving tray that contained two glasses of iced tea.

"Hey, guys. Enjoying this fabulous weather, I see."

Sam rose from one of the chaises. "Sugar lump! Wasn't expecting you."

She opened her mouth to reply, and nearly fainted when Joel Slade calmly rose from the next chaise, a glass of tea in his hand.

"Hello, Dixie. I've been hoping for a chance to talk to you." He held out the glass. "Vonnie, would you mind?"

"Not at all," Vonnie mumbled, reaching for the tumbler.

"Where's Clark?" Joel asked, feeling his way around the chaise toward Dixie.

"P-playing with some friends," Dixie managed.

Joel smiled, and in the instant before his hand latched on to her arm, she realized that he'd located her by the sound of her voice. "Excuse us," he said, towing her straight toward the house.

Dixie threw a helpless look at her parents, but they were too busy waggling their eyebrows at each other to notice. Joel put out his free hand and found the wall of the house, then he abruptly changed direction. It dawned on her where he was headed only a split second before they turned the corner. She heard him counting under his breath. When he got to ten, he stopped.

"That ought to do."

Suddenly she found her back against the rough cedar siding. "What—"

Before she could get out another word, he was kissing her!

After the initial shock of it, Dixie plastered herself against the house, but to deny that she participated in some way in that kiss would have been as impossible as denying the shivers that his unexpected kiss evoked or the tiny moan that escaped her when the kiss gentled and his hands tenderly cupped her face. Before breaking the kiss, however, he caged her with a hand planted on either side of her shoulders.

"Now," he said, pausing to inhale deeply, "we've established the first of two important facts."

"Which is?" Dixie croaked, clearing her throat afterward.

"That I am a blind man. Emphasis on the word *man.*"

Dixie was, to her shame, all too aware of Important Fact Number One.

"The second is that I do not appreciate and will not tolerate being treated like a handicapped child." He brought his nose up right next to hers and added, "Especially by a beautiful woman, which brings us right back to the first point, I believe."

Flustered, Dixie blurted the first thought that came to mind. "Don't think you can charm me. You don't even know what I look like!"

"Oh, but I do. My mother went out of her way to point you out to me before I enlisted. And one of the last things I saw before I lost my sight was a picture of you and Clark."

"What?"

"Mom sent it to me in a letter. I don't know who took it, but it was you in a hospital bed, wearing a pink top and holding your new baby."

Dixie caught her breath. She knew the exact photo he meant. She had insisted on brushing her hair, applying some lipstick and putting on a pink sweater to hide her hospital gown before the photo was snapped.

"Bess took it," she whispered.

"I had that photo and her letter in my pocket when we hit the IED," Joel revealed softly before pushing away from her. "So don't tell me I don't know what I'm talking about." He tapped his temple with one finger. "It's right here," he said. "And it always will be."

With that, he turned and left her, walking back the way they'd come. Only when he reached the end of wall did he reach out to orient himself, and then he rounded the corner and disappeared.

Tears sprang into Dixie's eyes. Though whether they were from watching Joel navigate blindly, that kiss or something else entirely, she didn't know.

She did know that she had wanted Mark in the picture that day, but he had taken a phone call instead, insisting that Bess take the shot without him. It hadn't seemed at all momentous at the time, but now…

Now, she had to wonder just what God was doing.

Chapter Four

Flipping through the television channels, Dixie sighed. One hundred and seventeen stations and she couldn't find a decent thing to watch. She supposed she might as well get ready for bed, not that she was sleepy by any means. The doorbell rang just as she got to her feet.

Puzzled as to who would be calling, Dixie went to take a cautious peek through the spy hole in her door. Her eyes went wide at the sight of Joel Slade standing on her sheltered doorstep. Her first thought was that he might be in trouble. What, after all, was a blind man doing out at night? Not that it was all *that* late. Frowning, she realized that she was discrediting him again, which still left her wondering why he was here. Then she thought of that kiss today. Of course. He must feel as bad about that now as she felt about the way she'd treated him earlier in the week. She opened the door.

"I know you're not lost."

One corner of his lips curled up, exposing the long, deep dimple in his cheek. "Can I come in?"

"Be my guest."

"Sorta the point," he said with a quick grin.

He carried his white cane extended to its full length and used it to find the threshold and step over it. At that point, she took his arm as she had seen his mother do, her own forearm paired with his.

"Here, let me help. I know you can manage, but this will be faster."

"Thank you." He pushed a button, collapsing the cane. "For the vote of confidence as well as the assistance."

She led him across the small foyer and into the spacious den, aware that he was counting steps. "How did you get here?"

He stopped, chuckling. "You've never heard of taxis? Or cell phone's with voice dial?"

"Ah."

"Great inventions, taxis and voice dial. I understand they've been around quite a while."

She laughed. "Okay, okay. I get the point." They proceeded on to the velvet-covered armchair that was her favorite. "Have a seat."

Watching him maneuver around to discover the chair and get himself into it, she backed up a few steps to the matching sofa and perched on the edge of the cushion. They sat in silence for several seconds before Dixie decided that she was being a poor hostess.

"I know you've come here to apologize," she said, "but it's not nec—"

"For what?" he interrupted. "That kiss?" He shook his head. "Sweetheart, if you're expecting an apology on that account, you've got a long wait coming. If anyone owes anyone an apology, you owe me. You weren't just condescending that day in the park, you were downright rude."

She opened her mouth to argue. Unfortunately, he was absolutely right. "I—I don't know what came over me that day. I have no excuse for my behavior, really. It's just…I'm not sure why, but you tend to make me very uncomfortable for some reason."

He grinned. "Okay." Sitting back, he crossed one ankle over the opposite knee. "Excellent, in fact. And another reason I won't be apologizing for that kiss."

Dixie's jaw dropped. He thought she was attracted to him!

Before she could come up with a way to dispute that, he changed the subject.

"Clark around?"

"Of course. Where else would he be at this hour?"

"Can I see him?"

Surprised, she answered, "He's asleep."

Joel blinked at that. "Goes down kind of early, doesn't he? Have you even had your dinner yet?"

"I had dinner over four hours ago."

"Four—" He sat bolt upright. "What time is it?"

Dixie glanced at the clock on the wall behind her. "Nineteen minutes past nine."

Joel slapped his hands to the top of his head before dropping them again to flip open the casing on his wristwatch and feel the dial with his fingers. "Good grief! I owe you an apology, after all. I thought it was just going six when I headed over here. It's this expensive Braille watch Mom bought me. I'm just not very good at reading it. Oh, man! Losing track of time is one of the worst things about being blind. I guess I need a watch that talks to me, but bless Mom's heart, she's done everything humanly possible to help me, and I don't want to offend her by not using the watch she gave me."

"Where is your mom?" Dixie asked sympathetically.

"Visiting one of my sisters in Oklahoma City. Natalie's expecting, you know. Should deliver tomorrow by C-section. Mom's gone to help out with the other two kids. I stayed here to study and keep out of everyone's way."

Dixie hadn't known about his sister's pregnancy or much of anything else about his family, but she didn't say so. She'd thought of Bess only in relation to her own mother and him—or rather, only in relation to herself. It seemed inexcusably self-centered now. She put on a smile, before remembering he couldn't see it, and asked, "Have you eaten? I can fix you something, if you like."

"Oh, I…" He shook his head, but then he smiled ruefully. "To tell you the truth, I was hoping for a meal when I came over here. I still haven't learned my way around Mom's kitchen all that well yet. Or any kitchen. I've never been much of a cook."

Dixie chuckled and rose. "Come on. You can keep me company while I heat some leftovers. Hope corn chowder and salad appeals. It's either that or mac and cheese."

"My grandma used to make sweet corn chowder," he said hopefully, getting to his feet.

"You're in luck then." She took his arm again, walked him around an ottoman off to one side and into the kitchen, leaving him at the round table. While she went to the refrigerator to take out the remains of her own dinner, he sat down. She chatted about nothing in particular while she started heating the chowder in the microwave. Then she dished up the salad and set it before him with a fork and napkin.

He dug right in, pausing after a moment to say, "Can I ask you a question?"

"A-all right," she answered tentatively.

"I've been wondering about that very first day in the park. If you didn't know it was me and you didn't know I was blind, why were you so shocked?"

"What makes you think I was shocked?"

"I heard it, felt it. I just can't come up with any good reason for it."

Dixie tried to decide what and how to tell him. Finally, she chuckled stiltedly. "You'll think it's weird."

"How so?"

She stirred the chowder and reprogrammed the microwave. "I—I'd been having this dream." She realized suddenly that she hadn't had the dream since first laying eyes on him, though what that might mean she couldn't imagine. The thick soup finished heating, and she delivered it to the table with a spoon. While he ate, she found herself telling him about the dreams, finishing with, "Then the tree actually fell during that last storm."

"Oh, wow. That…that was a couple days before we met in the park, wasn't it?"

"Yes. Yes, it was."

He scooped up a couple more bites, before saying, "This is really good."

"Thanks."

"Welcome." He waved his spoon. "Go on with your story. Has to be more to it. I mean, what does it all have to do with me and that first day in the park?"

Hooking the heels of her hands on the edge of the kitchen counter at her back, Dixie licked her lips. "The thing is, the guy in my dream, well…it was you."

He tilted his head and went utterly still for several seconds. Then he dropped the spoon, put both hands flat on the edge of the tabletop and stood.

For some reason, she gulped and rushed on. "Or someone a lot like you. I-isn't that funny?"

He stalked across the room, his hands twitching at his sides as if he fought to keep them there. "Funny? You think that's funny?" Suddenly, he was right in her face, his hands trapping hers on the edge of the counter. "God all but gives me to you in a dream, and you think it's a joke?"

Gives him to her? She gulped. "Dreams aren't real!"

"Didn't say they were. Are you saying God never communicates in dreams?"

"Not to me!"

"Bet Joseph thought the same thing, but when God told him in a dream to get up and take Jesus and Mary to Egypt, he did it."

"It's not the same thing!"

"Explain the tree falling."

"I told you, it was the storm."

"And God couldn't have a hand in that, right?"

She clamped her lips together because she couldn't argue that point.

"Okay," he whispered, sliding his arms around her. "Explain this."

Reason told her that the second kiss should be less of a shock, but in its own way it was even more shocking than the first. For one thing, it felt...completely reasonable, as right as her warming up a bowl of chowder for him. For another, there was just no way not to participate. She could no more *not* put her arms around him than she could *not* let her heart beat. Worst of all, it was the warmest, most delightful thing she'd experienced in far, far too long.

Was Joel right then? Was this, was he, what God intended for her?

She thought of the accident, of the way Mark had cartwheeled through the air, of waking in the hospital amazed to be alive and hoping, assuming, that he had also survived. If she could, why couldn't he? It wasn't fair that he had not survived.

Twisting away from Joel, she caught her breath, gasping, "This can't be! God wouldn't let Mark die, only to give me a handicapped husband."

The instant the words were out of her mouth, she wished them back. Joel backed away from her, shaking his head.

"Really? That's all you've got to say about it?" He thumped himself in the chest. "I may be handicapped, but I don't need you to take care of me, Dixie! And that's not what your problem is. You know what your real problem is? You don't trust God. You know the same as I do that we should be falling in love and getting married, but you're afraid to trust God with your future. That's what this is. So don't try to throw it back on me, baby!" Whirling on his heel, he marched straight out of the room, right through the open doorway.

Imagining him stomping all the way across the living room and smack into the wall, she rushed after him, but he turned three steps into the outer room, only to stumble over the ottoman.

Righting himself, he went on his way, Dixie anxiously trailing after. Not until he stepped onto the tile of the foyer did he put out his hands.

"Joel," she said pleadingly, not at all sure what she was asking for.

He found the door and located the knob. "And from now on don't put furniture in the middle of the floor!" he barked. Before she could point out that it wasn't in the middle of the floor, he yanked open the door, stepped through it and snapped it shut again.

Dixie looked at that closed door, and something turned over inside her chest. "From now on," he'd said, which meant that he'd closed that door on her just now but he hadn't closed it on *them.* That ought to have incensed or alarmed her, but she couldn't honestly say how she'd felt about it in that moment. One thing she did feel, however reluctantly, was admiration.

The man was at a terrible disadvantage, but he just didn't let it matter. Oh, he made accommodations. He wasn't so proud that he couldn't face reality—or so jaded that he didn't believe in dreams. And despite everything, he had faith—real, solid, unwavering faith, the sort of faith to make her feel small and foolish.

She heard his voice, and knew that he had probably called the taxi service again, which meant he'd be waiting out there all alone for some time yet. Sighing, she threw up a hand and went to join him.

Hearing the door open behind him, Joel thanked the dispatcher and got off the phone, stowing it in a pocket of his cargo pants. Handy things for a blind man, cargo pants. Dixie came out and sat down next to him on the single low step that led up to the entry of her house. The door was set back a few feet, providing a covered alcove where callers could wait, a nice arrangement in inclement weather.

Joel planted his feet and drew up his knees; balancing his

forearms atop them, he muttered, "I don't usually blow my temper like that."

A short silence followed, then she asked, "How can you believe we are meant to fall in love?"

He pushed his hands over his face, and told her, "You have your dream, Dixie, but I have a vision permanently planted inside my head."

"The photo, you mean."

"It's more than that," he said softly. "For years, ever since we moved to Lawton and my mother met your mother, she has believed that you are the girl for me."

Dixie snorted gently. "Yeah, I'm aware."

"She used to talk about you all the time. She'd say, 'Dixie will be old enough to car date in a few years,' and later, 'Dixie's as sweet as Vonnie,' and always, 'Dixie's pretty now, but she'll be beautiful one day.' Mom sure got that one right. She pointed you out to me once, walking across the church parking lot. You took my breath away. I'd have introduced myself to you then, but you weren't alone, and I figured that was as it should have been. But then when I saw that photo of you with some other guy's baby, it broke my heart." He chuckled ruefully.

"Joel, I—I don't know what to say."

"Nothing to say. It's nuts. All those years she kept going on about you, I listened and I watched, but I wasn't exactly waiting around, you know? Seemed like every time you were free, I was dating someone, or you were, but in the back of my mind I always thought there'd come a time when you'd be old enough, I'd call you and we'd go out. Then I enlisted, and you got married, and that was that."

"Until you lost your eyesight."

"Until I saw that photo," he corrected. "It was like a punch in the gut. Mom never stopped talking about you, reporting the little details of your life. I wished she wouldn't sometimes, but mostly I didn't really think about it. Then I opened that envelope and out dropped that photo, and my whole world just went right out of control. I felt like I'd been robbed. I didn't even read the letter, just crammed it into my pocket and stared at that picture until it was time to go out on patrol. I meant it when I said you were just about the last thing I ever saw or ever will see, you and Clark."

"But would that really have meant anything if you hadn't lost your eyesight?" she pressed.

He sighed. "Maybe you're right and it's just a blind man's dream, but I can't help thinking that God has something to do with it."

"To believe that is to believe that I was never supposed to marry Mark," Dixie refuted firmly, "and I can't accept that. It would mean that our love was false and Clark should never have been."

"I can't answer that, Dixie," Joel said quietly. "I'm ashamed to say that when I first heard your husband had died—right after I finally accepted that I was never going to see again—I thought it was some cruel, inhuman joke. I thought, 'Why now, when I have nothing left to offer her?' And then I thought, 'It should've been me. I'm the one who should've died.' That's one of the reasons I asked Mom not to tell you what had happened to me." He bowed his head.

"Oh, Joel. You shouldn't… It had nothing to do with you, believe me."

"I know. And eventually I came to understand that I'm just me without working eyes, and that's not a bad thing. A real inconvenient one, but not bad or hopeless."

"I'm glad about that," she whispered. "It's just, the idea of you and me… I guess I still don't know how to let go of Mark."

The taxi arrived, its wheels slowing and then scraping as it swung into the drive.

"Who asked you to?" Joel retorted, his anger rising again. He reminded himself that rejection hurt. Always had, always would. A simple fact that put no blame on her or his blindness. He got to his feet and pulled out his cane, sucking in a deep breath. "Sorry that I got the time mixed up and missed Clark," he said stiltedly, "but thanks for feeding me just the same."

"No problem."

"Be seeing you around." He chuckled ruefully at his own slip of the tongue. "Okay, I *won't* be seeing you, but I will be around if you change your mind."

She made no reply to that, but he hadn't expected her to. He stepped off toward the taxi, targeting it by the rumble of its engine and making certain his path was clear by sweeping the round tip of the cane over the ground in front of him.

Actually, he thought sadly, picturing her with baby Clark again, whether she changed her mind or not, he would *always* be seeing her.

Skipping church the following Sunday was cowardly, and Dixie knew it, but she just couldn't face Joel again, not after everything he'd revealed to her. Thinking back on Mother's Day, she realized that Joel's presence and Clark's infatuation with him had so distracted her from her memories that it had been a blessing in disguise. She'd made it through her first time back at the church that had been such a part of her life with Mark. She knew, in her heart of hearts, that she could finally go home again. To her surprise, she actually looked forward to doing so—if only it would not mean being thrown into constant proximity to Joel.

Guilt, her ever-present friend, had a part to play in that. She couldn't help feeling that she had somehow betrayed Mark with that second kiss. The first she could rationalize. She hadn't seen that coming in any way, but the last one… How could she find such pleasure, such satisfaction, such "rightness" in another man's kiss? It was bad enough that she'd caused her husband's death, robbed him of the chance to see their son grow up, but to feel something for another man seemed completely unacceptable.

Feel *something* she did, however. She just wasn't sure what that *something* might be. All she wanted to feel for Joel Slade was pity, and that, perversely, was the one thing she no longer felt for him.

The situation was entirely too confusing, and the worst part was that she couldn't talk to anybody about it. After all her complaints about Vonnie throwing Joel at her, she certainly couldn't confide in her mother. She dared not bring it up to any of her friends for fear that they would condemn her for her "betrayal" of Mark, make too much of Joel's revelations and her dream or think she'd lost her ever-loving mind because of the latter. Her dad would have a hard time not telling her mother, and her pastor…Dixie was ashamed to think how many times and in how many ways she had put off, ignored and avoided that poor man. She certainly wasn't comfortable dropping all this on him now.

No, the only place she could go with this was to her knees, but she found no answers there, none she could discern, anyway. More than once she had the passing thought that going to church might help with that. Yet, on Sunday, she stayed home. And brooded. She could feel the disappointment of her parents through the silence and distance.

She was relieved and doubly pleased when her dad showed up on Wednesday morning, chain saw in hand, to cut up that fallen tree. Not only was she glad to see a familiar face, but also, with the tree removed and the swing set repaired, she wouldn't have to take Clark to the park and worry about running into Joel.

The project veered into immediate difficulty, however. For one thing, the way the tree had fallen had created some odd angles and tight spots that were going to require a handsaw to manage, but Sam hadn't thought to bring along a handsaw. The other issue was Clark. He just could not understand why he couldn't help Pop-Pop, or at least be outside with him. When pleading and demanding didn't work, the little scamp actually tried to slip outside without his mother knowing it.

"I'm going to have to take him to Mom," Dixie told her sweaty father, standing before him with Clark on her hip while he gulped down the cold drink she'd brought him.

"I want Pop-Pop!" Clark wailed.

"You go on to Nana," Sam said, looking around at the mountains of debris he'd already whacked off the tree. "This isn't a safe place for you. Besides, I've got to haul off this little stuff so I have room to get at the big pieces. Once I get that cut up into firewood, I'll stack it over by the garage," he said to Dixie. "Make you some fine fires this winter."

"Thanks, Dad. What would I do without you?"

"Aw, you'd manage, I reckon," he rumbled when Dixie went up on her tiptoes to kiss his cheek. "What I haven't figured out yet," he said, changing the subject, "is how I'm going to get rid of the stump by myself." He waved that away. "One thing at a time. Listen, while you're at the house, go out to my workshop and get my big handsaw. It's on the wall to your left. Mom's got the key."

"Sure thing."

Clark renewed his wails when she moved off, reaching back over her shoulder for his grandfather. By the time they reached the car, he'd accepted that he wasn't going to get his way. When he saw his grandmother, he was all geared up for sympathy, clinging to Vonnie and sobbing in shuddering gasps.

"Little phony," Dixie chided indulgently, tapping him on the end of the nose. "You have fun, and I'll see you later." She thanked her mom, saying, "Don't let him con you into skipping his nap. After the morning he's put himself through, he's going to need it even more than usual."

"I won't," Vonnie promised. Then, just as Dixie was about to head out to the shop, Vonnie stopped her. "You should know something, Dix."

"What's that?"

"Joel is coming to lunch. I promised Bess I'd have him over anytime he chose, and he just called to say the pastor has offered him a ride out here today. Bess won't be back until tomorrow, and I imagine the pantry over there is pretty empty by now."

Dixie looked at her son and knew that he would be thrilled to see Joel again. Surprisingly, despite the way he'd shown his inner brat this morning, she didn't have it in her heart to deny him that. In fact, she was glad that they would have some time together, for both their sakes. She suspected Joel would enjoy Clark's company as much as Clark would delight in his, but she wouldn't have to see Joel herself.

"Well, that's fine, Mom," she said, trying to sound terribly casual about it all. "I trust Bess's new grandbaby is okay?"

"Why, yes, now that you mention it. Another little girl. Mommy and baby are home and doing well, which is why Bess feels she can drive home tomorrow."

"That's good," Dixie said, and got out of there before she had to explain how she even knew about the recent arrival. Of course, she had no way of being sure that Joel wouldn't spill the beans about everything himself, although if he hadn't done so already, she didn't think he would.

It seemed to her that her parents had certainly taken Joel Slade under their wing, but she supposed it was understandable, given Vonnie's close friendship with Bess and Joel's handicap. The Wallaces and Joel liked one another, that much was obvious, but a man his age wouldn't normally hang out with a couple old enough to be his parents unless he had special needs. Or was mature beyond his years. Or both. Dixie tried not to think that he might be hoping to run into her—and she especially tried not to be even a tiny bit thrilled about that possibility.

Sam Wallace was a man used to long hours of backbreaking labor, but he was not young anymore. Watching him drive himself, Dixie was ready for him to call a halt long before he seemed ready to give in. He had nothing to prove, after all.

"I'm not of a mind to wear a sawdust suit two days in a row," he told her the first time she suggested that he lay off for the afternoon. Then it was, "Never leave a job half done," followed by, "I've come this far. Not about to call it quits now," and finally, "One more cut, and I can start stacking."

That was when Dixie put her foot down. "You will do no such thing. Enough is enough."

Huffing for breath and wiping his brow, he finally conceded. "Okay, okay. The stacking can wait for tomorrow. Or the day after." He grinned and admitted, "Doubt I'll be able to get out of bed tomorrow."

Dixie rolled her eyes. "Men!"

"Uh-huh," he said, "but who did you call when you had a tree down? Wasn't Mom." With that, he cranked the chain saw. Dixie turned away, wanting as much distance between her and that last tree limb as she could get before the sawdust started flying again, not to mention the awful racket of the chain saw. She was almost to the back door when he screamed, the chain saw sputtering and dying before the horrific sound of his voice had even faded.

In a split second, the boat accident played through Dixie's mind. Even as she whirled and ran for her father, images from that day flashed in front of her. She saw Mark and the world churning and blood. But this time the blood was pouring out of her father's thigh.

"Dad!" She hit the ground on her hands and knees beside him.

"I dropped it!" He grabbed the flowing wound with trembling hands. "I just dropped it, Dixie!"

"We need help! Where's your cell phone?"

"Truck," he gasped. "Figured. Couldn't. Hear it. Stupid!"

"I'm getting help!" She jumped up again and ran for the telephone, ordering, "Keep pressure on that! Don't let go!"

She realized when she reached for the phone mounted on the kitchen wall that her own hands were bloody. But she hadn't even touched him! That meant blood had already spread over the ground next to him, and that was too much blood. Too much.

"Dear God in heaven," she began to pray as she dialed 911.

Somehow, she managed to hold it together and do what the dispatcher told her. Grabbing a stack of clean towels, her purse and cell phone, she ran back to her father, locking the door behind her. Relieved to find him still lucid, though in a great deal of pain, she wrapped a towel tightly around his injured leg. Next, she ran to unlock the gate. By the time she got back to Sam, he was tearing off his shirt.

"Get the water hose," he gasped out.

"What?"

"The water hose! I can't go to the hospital like this!"

She almost laughed, on the verge of hysteria. He was bleeding to death and he was worried about a little sawdust? Okay, a *lot* of sawdust. His chest was practically caked with it. They heard the sound of a siren in the distance.

"Hurry!" he ordered.

She got the water hose.

He was wet to the hips by the time the paramedics carried a gurney into the backyard, but together they'd managed to rinse off the worst of the sawdust. Dixie threw a clean towel across his shoulders as the paramedics examined him and used another to mop up herself. Every minute she prayed.

Please don't let him die. Please don't let the injury be permanent. Please let him be okay. He's such a good man, and he's loved You his whole life, Lord. He's such a good father, and he's loved me my whole life. He's such a good husband, and my mom would be lost without him. I know. Please take care of him. This time, Lord, please, please...

The emergency personnel were efficient, calm and authoritative. No one had to say that Sam was headed for the hospital, but Dixie was shocked when they told her that she couldn't ride in the ambulance.

"Policy," one of them stated firmly as two others carried Sam to the ambulance. "Besides," he added more gently, "we're going to be working to staunch the flow of blood, and we'll need all the room we have for that."

"Will he make it?" she wanted to know, trembling from head to toe.

"He needs a lot of stitching up, ma'am," was the careful answer.

Dixie gulped and nodded, then listened attentively to the pleasant young man's hurried directives. She wasn't to follow too close in her car, as far too many accidents happened that way. She should park only in designated areas of the hospital parking lot and enter the emergency room through a side door, not the ambulance entrance. She should give her name and her father's name at the front desk. They would call her back to be with him as soon as possible. Only after she'd checked in at the desk should she call anyone else. Whatever else she did, she was not to speed, drive recklessly or attempt to make calls on her cell phone while driving.

"Don't want to have to make a return trip for you," the EMT said with a tight smile.

Obediently, Dixie nodded her understanding and pulled her keys from her purse. The ambulance was well down the street, sirens blaring, before she even got her car out of the garage.

Crying quietly, she managed to keep the ambulance in sight along the route to the hospital, whispering the same litany over and over again all the while.

"Please, Lord. Whatever You will…whatever You need from me. Please, Lord."

Chapter Five

Sam's jaw clenched against the pain as the doctor closed the pressure bandage.

"Too much repair to manage in here," he said. "We're waiting for an operating room to clear. That way we can put him under before we give it another good cleaning and stitch the wound."

Dixie clutched her father's hand and asked the question they were both afraid to have answered. "Is he going to be all right?"

"He's lost some tissue, but the muscle doesn't appear too badly damaged, so I don't think he'll lose any function. Luckily, it's on the outside of his thigh."

"Luck," Sam rasped, "has nothing to do with it."

"A large, ugly scar and several weeks of recovery should be the worst of it, but don't be surprised if he has to have some physical therapy," the doctor went on.

Dixie heaved a sigh of relief. "Thank you."

"He's a tough old buzzard," the younger man replied with a smile. "I'd have passed out a long time ago."

Sam chuckled and gasped, "And miss all the attention?"

"You've got about five more minutes to enjoy it," the doctor said, sweeping from the small, cell-like room.

Sam moaned, muttering, "Where's Mom? Should've been here by now."

"I'll go check. Be right back."

Patting his shoulder with one hand, she clutched her cell phone with the other, intending to run out into the waiting area so she could call her mother again. Vonnie had needed to drop off Clark at a neighbor's before she could make the dash into town. Dixie hurried from the cubicle.

"Here you are. On your left." The nurse accompanying Joel stepped back.

"Thank you," Joel said, a millisecond before a soft, curvy body collided with his.

"Oof!"

"Dixie!" He knew instinctively that she'd been rushing from Sam's bedside when she'd literally bumped into him. Alarm shot through him, and he slid his hands over her shoulders and back, trying to discern her emotional and physical state. "What's wrong? Is Sam all right? Are you all right?"

Her hands fisted in the sides of his shirt, and for an instant he thought she might lean against him, embrace him, even, but she let go and pulled back a few inches.

"He will be. They're taking him into surgery any minute, though, and he wants to see Mom. Where is she?"

"She's parking the car. Can I speak to him?"

"Of course. He's still in some pain, though. They're giving him blood, and they've set up a nerve block, but they don't want too many drugs in his system because they're going to put him under to stitch him up."

"I understand." She turned to lead the way, but instead of taking her arm, Joel slung his around her shoulders. He wanted her close just now, and he had the feeling that she needed the support. They moved forward several steps.

"Joel," Sam growled. "You didn't have to come."

Joel smiled, relieved to hear his friend's voice, despite the tone of pain. "Oh, but I did." He explained about inviting himself to lunch and catching a ride out to the Wallace place with the pastor, who had been on his way to Duncan. "After Dixie called, I rode back in with Vonnie. And to think I complained about missing you," he noted wryly. "All in all, I think I'd have preferred that to this."

"Me, too!"

They both chuckled, though Sam's laugh sounded rough and mirthless. Joel liked Sam, admired him. Compared to his own father, who had disappeared years ago without so much as a word to his wife and children since, Sam was a hero, a real man who took his obligations seriously but wasn't afraid to show love and friendship. It grieved Joel to hear the pain in his voice when Sam asked, "Where is she?"

No one had to ask who "she" was.

"Parking the—"

Vonnie blew into the space before he could finish. "I'm here! Samuel Wallace, what have you done?"

"Eh. Not as strong as I used to be. Arm got tired, dropped down while the chain saw was running. Simple as that."

While her mother clucked over her father, Dixie quickly explained what the doctor had told them.

"Thank God!" Vonnie exclaimed, her voice sounding muffled. Joel imagined that she was hiding her face behind her hands or perhaps hugging Sam. She was definitely turned away.

"Actually," he said, sharing her relief at what was mostly good news, "that's an excellent idea. Thanking God, I mean. Would anyone mind if we took a minute so I could lead us in prayer?"

"Please do," Sam rasped.

Nodding, Joel eased forward, realizing only then that he still had his arm about Dixie's shoulders. She slipped free, linking her hand to his. Realizing that she'd stretched out, he lifted his other hand and felt Vonnie's grip it. Assuming that the women were linked to Sam, Joel bowed his head.

"Most gracious Lord God, we thank You for sparing Sam from permanent injury. Ease his pain now, Father, and in the weeks to come as he heals. Keep Your protective hand upon him and guide the physicians as they repair the damage. Restore him, Lord, to full function and full health. The glory and honor for his healing and every other good thing is Yours, Lord, and never let us forget it. In the name of Your Holy Son, amen."

He heard a sniff from Dixie and squeezed her hand. She squeezed back before letting go. Joel's heart swelled. Perhaps friendship was all they'd ever have between them, but that was more than he'd feared they could have after their last meeting, even if it was less than he wanted. He'd been over and over it in his mind. A part of him feared that his mother's influence and his own blindness was all there was to his feelings for Dixie. Bess had declared Dixie the girl for him, and hers had been all but the last face he'd seen before the explosion and the ensuing darkness. He couldn't deny that he'd obsessed over that a good bit. Why Dixie? Why that particular photo?

On the other hand, if he was going to hold one beautiful face before his mind's eye for the rest of his life, why not Dixie's? Was he wrong to think that God had singled her out for him? He'd tried not to spin dreams, to make assumptions, to limit God in any way, but then she'd told him about her amazing dream, and it had seemed so very obvious that they belonged together, that they were meant to be. But even if that was God's plan, and not just his own blind obsession, who was to say when it came into being? Before Mark's death? After? Was it God's perfect will or Plan B? And what if Dixie never saw it that way?

Joel didn't have the answers. He didn't know why he and Dixie couldn't have gotten together from the beginning, or why Mark had died and he had lost his eyesight. He didn't know if Dixie would ever adjust to her loss and be ready to move on with her life, to love again. If not, then he had to believe that God would have someone else for him, because he definitely did not want to spend his life alone in the dark.

Then again, he was never alone. He had begun to actually feel God's presence in the hospital after the explosion. Trembling in fear, raging in anger, horrified at his loss, confused with his surroundings, he had begun to sense, within himself and apart from the chaos, that Greater One Whom he had accepted as a boy. He wished he had felt God's physical presence sooner, that it had been more real to him before he'd lost his eyesight, but he had been more blind then than now.

Sam began to grouse about not getting the wood stacked. Apparently, he'd cut the fallen tree into logs for a wood-burning fireplace. Joel hadn't even realized that Dixie had one, though it made sense. Most newer homes did these days. He thought about how nice it would be to sit before a crackling fire with Dixie snuggled against him, Clark playing quietly on the rug at their feet. He wished, suddenly, that he could see Clark, really know what he looked like now. His mother had told him to picture himself at that age but with curls. Joel was afraid to do it. That would make Clark seem too much like his own son. That would be risking too much of his heart if Dixie never came to care for him.

Sam grumbled about the stump in Dixie's backyard, and Joel knew that it was just a way to keep his mind off his pain. Nevertheless, he quickly sought to reassure the older man.

"Don't worry about any of that," he said, hearing footsteps in the passageway outside. "I'll get over to Dixie's and stack the wood. We can deal with the stump later."

Suddenly, Dixie's hand grasped his arm and gently towed him out of the way as someone entered the space, several someones, actually.

"Okay, Paul Bunyan," a woman's cheery voice said, "let's get you sewed up. You folks can wait in the family lounge." While metal parts clanked and clunked, she told them how to get there.

"Doc will be out to talk to you as soon as he's finished. Then someone will come and get you when the lumberjack here is out of recovery and heading for a room." Wheels whirred and screeched on slick flooring as she spoke.

"Careful," a man said, and then they were out of the space. Joel heard the nurse joking with Sam as they wheeled him away.

"Didn't anyone ever tell you juggling chain saws is dangerous?"

"There goes my plan to join the circus," Sam rumbled, and Joel chuckled.

"Thank God you were with him," Vonnie said, momentarily throwing Joel off-kilter.

"But I wasn't," Dixie replied shakily, "not all the time. I left him there alone when I brought Clark to you!"

"You were there when it counted," Joel remarked soothingly, reaching out for her. He wondered if she even knew what she was doing when she stepped forward and let him slide his arm around her back.

"Joel's right," Vonnie said, sniffing. "He'd have bled to death if you hadn't acted so quickly."

"At least I was able to do something this time," Dixie whispered, and Joel knew that she was thinking of Mark's death. Would she ever get past that loss and trauma? He could only pray so.

"Let's find that lounge," he said. "I, for one, could use a cup of coffee."

It took far longer than Dixie expected. Two interminable hours passed before the doctor came out to report.

"Everything went fine," he assured them, standing before them in the large, homey lounge, "but we had to be sure that the muscle was completely intact, and that the bone wasn't cracked or broken by the impact of the chain saw. Luckily, it seemed to be a glancing blow."

"Don't think it was luck," Joel said from a chair beside her.

Dixie's attention zipped to Joel's face, even as the physician targeted him with a curious look, observing, "Mr. Wallace said the same thing earlier."

Joel smiled. "Not surprised. Our faith teaches that God watches over us and works everything in our lives to our benefit."

The doctor shifted his weight, tilting his head. "You're blind, aren't you?"

"I am. Concussive trauma."

"And you think that's for your benefit?" the doctor asked in an amazed tone.

Joel's answer came without hesitation. "I do."

"How so?"

"I don't know. If I hadn't lost my sight I'd still be in the Marine Corps. I might have died of war wounds or a training accident. I might never have come home, never gone back to college, never thought about law school…any number of things. Look, God didn't plant a bomb in the road. Some bad guy did that. My vehicle hit it. Doesn't matter to me why God allowed that. I only have to trust that He'll work it to my good."

Dixie stared at Joel. The words of Romans 8:28 rolled through her mind.

"And we know that in all things God works for the good of those who love Him, who have been called according to His purpose."

Not long after Mark's death, someone had quoted that verse to her. It had infuriated her. She'd thought that they were saying that Mark's death was a good thing, that God had engineered it in order to bless her. But she didn't want to be blessed from such tragedy! How dared God do such a thing.

But maybe that was not how it worked.

Maybe God allowed certain circumstances to unfold as someone else arranged them, purposefully or unknowingly, for His own reasons. Maybe that way lay the greater good. And maybe not. She didn't know anymore. Still, if Joel and Romans 8:28 were right, she could trust God to work for her good. Couldn't she?

It was hard to see how anything good could come out of Mark's death, but much good had come out of his life. Clark, for one thing. And good things could still come her way. If she would let them.

The doctor smiled and said, "Admirable attitude."

"More a matter of faith, really," Joel said.

"Then I admire your faith."

"Better to admire my Lord," Joel replied with a smile. "Faith in the wrong thing accomplishes nothing."

"Let me guess," the doctor said, eyes slitting. "You're going to be a preacher."

"Lawyer."

The doctor laughed. "You'll make a good one. Very persuasive."

"Be glad to persuade you a little more," Joel said. "Anytime you want." He put out his hand. "Name's Joel Slade, by the way."

The two shook hands. "I just might take you up on that, Joel."

Before he swept from the room, he told them that someone would be along to get them when Sam woke up from the anesthetic. Dixie stared at Joel with new respect, sad humility and not a little pride.

Another hour crawled by. Dixie had already checked on Clark earlier and been told that he was happily playing with the two young children in the household of her mother's neighbor. Both were older than Clark, but Dixie knew the family well from years of acquaintance. No doubt he'd be worn-out and cranky by the time she got him home again, but she'd deal with that later. Right now, she just wanted to see her father and know that his pain had lessened. Her mother's tension would fade then, and Dixie could finally relax.

Joel provided distraction, making conversation, offering suggestions. At times, he sat in silent prayer. Other times, his lightest touch warmed and comforted her, an arm stretched out behind her, a hand brushing hers, the playful bump of shoulders, a friendly pat. This wasn't the first time, Dixie recalled, that Joel's presence had distracted her from her anxiety. This time she appreciated that fact.

At last, a nurse in scrubs appeared in the lounge.

"Sam Wallace's family?"

Both Vonnie and Dixie rose. Halfway across the floor Dixie realized that Joel hadn't moved from his chair. She went back to him.

"You coming?"

He spread his hands. "I can wait here."

Can. She didn't know what that meant. "Well…if you want."

He shifted uncomfortably. "Actually, I don't need to wait. I should call a taxi and get someone to point me toward the main entrance."

That certainly didn't seem right. Dixie bit her lip and glanced at her mom, before reaching down for his hand. "Come on."

"I'm not family," he said quietly, his long fingers wrapping tightly around hers.

She felt as if she'd been kicked in the chest. It was true. He wasn't family. Mark had been family, and in a just world it would be Mark sitting there, Mark holding her hand, Mark praying at her father's bedside, not Joel. But none of that was Joel's fault. She could not blame him for Mark not being here. She had only herself to blame for that.

Suddenly the fact that she wanted Joel there, that he had been a comfort and a support to her, seemed a betrayal of Mark. Still, she couldn't escape the knowledge that Joel's obvious fondness of Sam and concern for his well-being had been a comfort to her and her parents. Besides, Joel had waited with them all this time; he deserved the chance to put his mind at ease where Sam was concerned.

"Dad will want to see you," she told him, tugging on his hand. Instead of releasing her, he let her pull him to his feet.

"I want to see him, too."

"Well, then, let's go."

Vonnie and the nurse led off as soon they saw Dixie and Joel following.

"I just don't want to intrude any more than I already have," Joel said softly, even as he kept pace with her.

Dixie shook her head. "We've taken hours of your time. You're not intruding."

He clapped a hand down over her forearm. "You haven't taken anything. I want to be here. I want to be here for you and your parents, Dixie."

She felt a flutter of pleasure inside her chest. Dismayed, she asked herself why Joel had to be so attractive. Despite his blindness, the man packed a real wallop in the appeal department. It didn't seem fair. He was equal parts honesty and charm, confidence and caring and entirely too handsome.

Mark had also been handsome, of course, she thought loyally, picturing his lanky, boyish frame and even, symmetrical features. She remembered his sweetness and willingness to please, his quiet, easygoing nature.

A truth she had long avoided struck her. Mark had been too easygoing, too easy to please. He hadn't liked to stand up for himself, and she had taken advantage of that. How many times, she wondered, had he given in to what she wanted, what she thought best, when his own judgment had been contrary to hers?

Joel Slade would never let her get away with that. Joel would never let anyone or anything override his better judgment in important matters. He would yield, yes, if shown the error of his thinking. He would compromise when he could find a way, even indulge others when he felt he could, but rarely would he concede on any important matter without a fight. She knew that about him as well as she knew it about herself.

And his blindness had nothing to say about it.

She felt sorry for his handicap, but the idea of Joel as an object of pity was laughable to her now. Maybe he needed a little assistance at times, but he certainly wasn't helpless. She remembered him marching her around the corner of the house that day and how he'd made his point. She thought how he'd earlier told her father not to worry, that he would stack the firewood in Dixie's backyard and help Sam figure out what to do about the stump later. Thinking of the calm, engaging, self-assured manner in which he'd witnessed to the doctor, she concluded that the doc was right. Joel would make an excellent attorney, just as he had, no doubt, made an excellent Marine. No, not helpless at all.

Joel Slade was blind, but his intelligence, character, compassion, personal strength and the depth of his faith made him a man more capable than most. They made him the sort of man, in fact, with whom a woman could spend her life. Not that she was necessarily that woman, of course. Still, she couldn't help liking him, admiring him, wanting to be his friend.

"Forget the taxi," she said, making a sudden decision. "I'll drive you home."

Joel nodded, fighting to keep his expression pleasantly bland. *At least it's a step forward,* he thought. Whether or not it was a step toward his heart's desire, he had no way of knowing, but it was definitely progress. As they journeyed through the hospital, he thought of the dream Dixie had described to him, and smiled. She might as well have described his dream as hers, for he truly wanted nothing more than to be there for her and Clark, as he wanted to be there for all those he loved.

Loved.

He'd known, early on, that he probably loved the idea of Dixie more than Dixie herself, but that was no longer so. She might be wrong about something, but until convinced otherwise, she'd fight on. He liked that about her. He didn't even care, at this point, how much convincing she might take. As for himself, he'd never been so sure of anything in his life. He'd tried not to be. It hadn't seemed smart to be so easily convinced that she was the one for him, but he just couldn't escape the conclusion.

He gripped her hand in his, felt her warm presence at his side, inhaled her perfume, felt the gentle gust of her breath as she turned her head to speak to him, heard the sound and timbre of her voice, and he ached to call her his. He wanted her to belong to him and vice versa. He wanted the same with Clark, the right to be with him, care for him, play with him, parent him. Joel wanted a rich and full life for all three of them. Together.

Most of all, though, Joel wanted Dixie and Clark to be happy, with or without him.

So, yes, he loved her and her son.

Turning, they pushed through a heavy door into a quiet, slightly chilly, clean-smelling room. Joel grinned, hearing Vonnie laugh and Sam, still half-asleep and slurring his words, assure everyone that he was, "Fine. Fine. Ne'er be'er."

He even, Joel thought, loved Dixie's parents. They were salt-of-the-earth people, as dedicated to one another and their family as it was possible for a couple to be, and no one had ever been kinder or more welcoming to him.

"How many stitches, tough guy?" he asked, knowing that was something Sam would want to brag about.

"Seventy-five!" Sam announced proudly. "Top that!"

"Oh, good grief," Vonnie scolded, fondness underlying every syllable. "Men! If I don't watch you, you'll be running around in shorts to show off the scars."

"'At's right," Sam slurred. "Gordy Blevins's always braggin' 'bout twenty-six in 'is arm. Ha! Piker."

Vonnie clucked, and Dixie snorted, but Joel just grinned all the wider. "More power to you, I say."

"Now, don't encourage him," Vonnie retorted. "He'll be slicing up the other thigh just for attention."

"I'll passh on 'at," Sam muttered.

"You sound like you need to sleep," Joel said, inching over to the bed and holding out his hand. Sam's tough, leathery fingers caught his and squeezed.

"Thangs for comin', Joem. Take care m'shugar lump, uh?"

"Hey, don't worry about it," Joel said noncommittally, wondering how Dixie was taking that. To his surprise, her hand patted his shoulder, then she edged him aside.

"Sleep well, Daddy. I'm so sorry about this."

"My own faul', shugar, but 's all good now."

"The doctor says we can go home tomorrow," Vonnie told him.

Sam's answer was nothing more than a low hum, followed by a snore. Joel felt Dixie's arm slide through his. She turned him, and they tiptoed out into the hall, Vonnie with them.

"Mom, I'm going to run Joel home, but I'll come back to sit with you and Dad."

"I can take a taxi," Joel reluctantly volunteered, working to keep his tone casual. "Do it all the time."

"No, no," Vonnie said firmly. "You two pick up Clark and get a bite to eat. The nurse has already ordered a late meal for your father and me. I threw some things in a bag before we left the house, so I'm fine for the night. I'll call you in the morning or if anything changes, but I don't expect a spot of trouble, not one. Now go."

He heard a smack and then felt a kiss pressed noisily to his own cheek. Dixie argued half-heartedly, but they were on their way in only moments. Joel relaxed and let himself be led, without bothering to count steps or otherwise try to note his surroundings. The place was a confusing maze of corridors and turns, but he didn't care, not with Dixie holding on to him.

"You must be hungry," he said after a bit.

"I didn't even think about food until Mom mentioned it just now," Dixie replied, "but now that the subject has come up, I'm starving."

"That makes two of us. How do you feel about a burger at the local drive-thru? You're driving so I'm buying."

"Sounds good, but would you mind if we picked up Clark first? He's never been with anyone but family this long."

"I'd prefer it, frankly. He's a great kid, Dixie. I was delighted to spend time with him at your mom's. That's quite a playroom they've set up for him."

Dixie burst out laughing. "So you made it to the playroom, did you?"

"Are you kidding? We ate our lunch in there, all three of us at that little table with those itty-bitty chairs. It's surprisingly difficult to eat when your knees keep getting in the way. Clark laughed his head off." Dixie did, too, and the sound of her amusement thrilled Joel all the way to his toes.

"Now, that I'd have paid to see," she chortled.

"Repeat performance anytime you like," he promised, and he meant it wholeheartedly. "Free of charge." Unless, of course, she preferred to pay with her heart.

Chapter Six

"You're crying."

Silence had descended on Dixie's car the moment they'd left the parking lot, bringing with it emotions that she had not expected. She supposed it was the letdown after the crisis. Now that the worst was past, she had time to acknowledge the fears that had driven her for all those hours.

Taking her eyes off the road just long enough to glance at Joel, Dixie smiled through her tears. He lounged in the passenger seat as if he did not have a worry in the world. She would not have been nearly so sanguine. To sit in the dark while someone else literally held your life in her hands, which is what happened every time you got into a car that you weren't driving yourself, seemed like a very frightening experience to her. But then he turned out to be more aware than she'd imagined. She had been so careful to keep silent, not to sob or even sniff.

"How did you know?"

"The way you're breathing."

"You can actually hear my breath?"

"Every moment I'm with you."

She shook her head and wiped at the tear streaks on her face. "You never cease to amaze me, Joel."

"I can tell you're crying. I can't tell why."

Dixie sighed. "I don't know, really. It's just…the accident wouldn't have happened if Dad hadn't been there to help me." Her voice spun out to a tiny, grimacing squeal.

Joel shifted in his seat. "Your father's accident is not your fault, Dixie. He said it himself. He pushed himself too far and got too tired to hold up the chain saw. Besides, he's going to be fine."

"Mark wasn't," she whispered.

Joel sat back, tilting his head. "Is that what this is about? You're remembering the other accident? That was unspeakably tragic, but it wasn't any more your fault than this was."

"But it was!" she blurted, suddenly sobbing. "It was."

Joel braced a hand on the dashboard, calmly ordering, "Pull over, babe. Find a place and pull over."

She did, turning into a strip mall on the edge of town. Catching her breath, she scrubbed at her eyes. "I'm sorry. Don't know what came over me."

"Listen to me," he said, searching for and finding her hand. "It's been a long, emotionally trying day, and it's brought up bad memories from the past. I know exactly what that's like. You're due a good cry, if you want. But you are not responsible, not for Sam's accident and not for Mark's."

But she was. Suddenly, it seemed paramount that someone know it, that Joel know it.

"You're wrong," she whispered. "I am responsible for the accident that killed my husband."

Joel shook his head. "That can't be, honey. You obviously feel responsible, but—"

"He wanted a boat," she interrupted, fresh tears pouring from her eyes. "A *new* boat, and he deserved it. Mark never spent money on himself, not like most people, but he wanted that boat." She gulped and confessed, "I wanted a new dining-room set. So when he showed me the cost of a new boat, I insisted that he test a used one instead."

"Dixie," Joel said softly, "that doesn't make it your fault."

"I even found the boat and made the appointment," she went on in a quavering voice. "The owner was a salvager who restores used boats on the side. I should have known it was dangerous."

"Dixie."

"He made us sign a waiver, Joel! Before he would even let us take the boat out, he made us sign a release. I should have known something would go wrong."

Joel's hand touched the top of her head and slid down to her nape. "If you should have known, then Mark should have known, too," he said reasonably. "Did he say anything about it?"

"No, but—"

"Well, then, there you are. What exactly happened, anyway?"

She shook her head. "Something went wrong with the steering. It was an inboard motor, but that's all I know about boats. By the time we realized we had a problem, it was too late. We hit a concrete pylon for a lake pier that they were refurbishing."

"How fast?" Joel asked. She blinked, trying to think, and he shook her gently with the hand at her nape. "How fast was the boat going when it hit the pylon, Dixie?"

"I—I don't know. Fast."

"And were you behind the wheel?"

"No."

"No," he echoed. "Mark was at the wheel of an unfamiliar boat, and it was going fast. If it had been going slower, you might have both survived, so why isn't it Mark's fault?"

"B-because…" She'd never thought of it that way, and she wasn't going to. "You can't blame him!"

"You're right," Joel said. "I can't blame him any more than I can blame you."

Dixie thought about that for a long time because he'd given her a whole new perspective. But letting go of the guilt was hard because it meant letting go of so much else—like her reason for staying stuck in her grief and not getting on with her life.

"You don't understand," she mumbled.

Joel massaged the nape of her neck. "Oh, baby, do I ever understand. Want to know how many of my company died while I was in Iraq? Ninety. Two from my own squad. The day we hit the IED, four from our company gave their lives. Not their eyes, their lives. Honey, you can't tell me anything about survivor's guilt. Been there. Done that."

"Oh, Joel."

"Know how I beat it? When I was going through rehab, a chaplain told me that by questioning my own survival, I was proclaiming my lack of faith in my Lord and Savior. He pretty much told me the same thing earlier when I was mad at God for losing my eyesight. I just didn't get it then."

"B-but you seem so accepting now."

"Now. At the time, I was anything but. It was a year before I could accept the blindness, Dixie, the most miserable year of my life. Only after I went to my knees and gave my anger to God did it all start to make sense and come right."

Dixie stared at him, openmouthed. The dream. The dream had changed when she'd confessed her anger to God. It went from the tree falling on the swing set with Clark on it, to Joel being there and rescuing Clark. Did that mean that things were starting to "come right" in her life? Except…wait. Joel hadn't rescued Clark so much as shown her that he was all right. Then, in the last dream, Joel had led Clark away. She pictured the scene, the two of them walking down the street, Joel's hand on Clark's shoulder, and suddenly it was if a lightning bolt hit her. Joel hadn't been leading Clark away; Clark had been guiding him! A boy guiding his blind father.

But what about Mark? He was Clark's father. How could she allow him to be replaced?

"I'm so confused."

Joel dropped his hand and released his seat belt. Sliding his arm across her shoulders, he leaned close and brought his head to hers, pressing a kiss to her temple. "Give it time, sweetheart. Like I said, the first year was a mess. The second year, well, that was a revelation, and now…now every day feels like an adventure."

The second year. Dixie caught her breath. "You were already blind when Mark died."

"Yes."

"I can't believe I never knew."

"I didn't want anyone to know at first. Couldn't bear the thought of anyone else feeling as sorry for me as I felt for myself."

She smiled and brushed a palm across his cheek. "You still can't tolerate pity."

He chuckled. "At least I'm still not wallowing in self-pity."

"For the record," she told him softly, "I don't feel sorry for you. I admire you, Joel. You've handled your situation so much better than I've handled mine."

"Not the same thing," he told her. "Your kind of loss is more devastating. After your husband died, I asked my mom specifically not to tell you about my blindness, partly because I just didn't want you burdened with that knowledge. And partly because of my pride," he confessed.

"You have a right to your pride, Joel."

"I'd like to think so, but mostly I just didn't want you to think of me as less than a whole man. You see, Dix, my mom isn't the only one who believes that you're the right woman for me."

Warmth spread through her, filling all the cold recesses in her heart, and yet…

"Joel, I wish I could say that I believe it, too."

He slid back into his seat. "So do I, because until you do, it's hopeless."

She heard the sadness and disappointment beneath his warm, even tone, and it pierced her heart. "I—I just don't know how," she whispered.

He nodded. "I understand. I really do." He fumbled for and found the safety belt. Pulling it across himself, he located the clasp and fastened it. "Clark's waiting," he said with a smile, "and I've gone right past hungry to don't-get-too-close-I-might-take-a-bite-out-of-you."

She laughed, grateful for the teasing as it lightened the mood.

"Let's get on the road, then."

After quickly scrubbing her hands over her face, she put the car in motion again. Ten minutes later, she lowered a sleepy Clark into his safety seat and buckled him in.

"Joe!" he said happily.

Joel reached back, and Clark caught his hand.

"Hey, pal! Did you have fun?"

Clark nodded and babbled something about trucks and cheese sandwiches. Ten minutes after that, he had dropped off to sleep. He continued to sleep, even when Dixie pulled into the drive-thru and ordered cheeseburgers for herself and Joel. He slept while Joel wolfed down his burger and had a chocolate milkshake for dessert. He slumbered on through the mundane conversation and the light laughter and the drive to Bess's house.

"Good night, Dixie," Joel said against the background of Clark's contented, velvety breaths. "I just want you to know one thing."

"What's that?"

He gripped her hand. "I'm going to pray for you."

"Thank you, Joel."

"No, not like that. I've been praying for your welfare since Mark died. This is purely selfish."

"I—I don't understand."

"I once told you that I believe God gave me to you in a dream. Well, maybe that's not enough, so now I intend to ask God to give *you* to *me*. Only seems fair."

Dixie smiled tremulously. That was perhaps the sweetest, most romantic thing anyone had ever said to her. What could she possibly say to something like that? Lifting her hand, she laid it against his cheek, feeling the prickle of his beard. Clark, she thought fondly, would be entranced. She couldn't help being a bit entranced herself.

He caught her hand, turned his face and left a kiss in her palm before getting out of the car. "Good night, sweetheart," he said through the open door. "I'd ask you to dream of me, but you already have."

Stunned, Dixie burbled with laughter that seemed just on the verge of tears as she watched him stroll up the path to his mother's front door. He couldn't see the colorful azaleas and peonies that flanked the paved walkway or the dark green door at the top of the steps of the small frame house, but she had no doubt that he was aware of them. None at all. Or that he meant exactly what he'd said. He intended to ask God for her.

In some ways that terrified her. In other ways, she was oddly glad about it. On the one hand, how could she be "given" to anyone if she refused to first let go of Mark? On the other, what was she really holding on to? A memory? A ghost? Guilt? What exactly, she wondered, was she so afraid of?

"Father, forgive me," she whispered, feeling a glow begin in her heart, "for my lack of faith. Show me how to believe in Your abundant blessings, not just in my own loss. I want to believe that You can give me love in a dream. But only if it's true."

Dixie couldn't stop thinking about all that Joel had said. She went over in her mind his every word and action since she'd first laid eyes on him that day in the park, when neither of them had known the other's identity. She prayed to fully understand that dream and any significance it might have, as well as all that had happened since.

As she lay in her solitary bed that night, her mind moved ceaselessly but gently from point to point, like the graceful, ephemeral dance of a jellyfish through still water, never slowing or rushing but constantly wafting toward some unknown destination. She rose the next morning feeling strangely rested, despite precious little sleep, and went about her day with smooth efficiency, caring for Clark and the house and the bills, talking to her parents on the phone and arranging for a friend of her dad's to pick up and deliver Sam's truck back to the Wallace place.

After Sam was home from the hospital and settled comfortably in his recliner in front of the TV, she drove over with Clark so the two could spend a little time together while she chatted with her mother in the kitchen. Vonnie was full of information.

"The pastor came by the hospital this morning."

"Not surprised."

"He was very relieved to hear that we were just waiting for discharge instructions so we could head home. He apologized and apologized for not being around when the accident happened."

"That's nice."

"Speaking of nice, that nice young doctor referred Sam to a wound-care specialist. Just a precaution, but helpful, I think."

"Yes, I can see how it would be."

"It could have been much worse, but it's not just your run-of-the-mill injury. We had to fill three prescriptions on our way home. Let's see, antibiotic, pain relief. I think the third is for inflammation or something."

Dixie nodded. Tears pricked her eyes as the terror rushed back over her. "I thought Dad was going to bleed to death!"

Vonnie flew around the counter and folded Dixie in her arms. "Oh, sweetie. After all you've been through, I don't know how you managed. Your father and I talked about it last night. He said you were clearly shaken, but you kept your cool and did all the right things. He's so proud of you, Dixie. We both are. You saved his life, do you know that? The big idiot left his cell phone in the truck! Said he didn't want to take a chance on losing or breaking it and didn't figure he'd be able to hear it over the sound of the saw, anyway." She cupped Dixie's face in her hands. "If you hadn't been there at that moment... You saved him, Dixie. You saved him."

Dixie sucked in a deep breath and closed her eyes. "I'm so glad." She looked her mother in the face then. "It did bring everything with Mark back. I relived the other accident again, but even as it all flashed by me, I knew that I had to help Dad—and that I couldn't have helped Mark. I guess, in the back of my mind, I always thought that I should have been able to do something that day."

Wordlessly, Vonnie hugged Dixie close. Mother and daughter clung to each other for a long time. Finally, they broke apart, both dabbing at their eyes. Vonnie picked up with her chatter again in an obvious attempt to lighten the mood.

"Bess called. I told her there wasn't a thing she could do here, so she's delayed her return for another day."

"Problems?" Dixie asked, sniffing back the last of her tears.

"One of the older grandchildren was running a slight temperature last night. Doesn't seem to be anything serious."

Vonnie went on, talking about this and that. Not one word was said about Joel.

It didn't feel right, like all those times after Mark's death when everyone around Dixie had chatted so brightly on so many subjects except the one consuming all the air in the room. She had reacted with anger and tears back then, accusing them of wanting to forget Mark and then sobbing when they did talk about him. Her grief had been fresh and sharp at the time, but lately it had begun to feel old and tired.

Dixie shook her head. All her angst about letting go of Mark seemed rather foolish suddenly. No one really had a choice about that. Death severed all physical ties. Distance and time gradually pulled the emotional link to a fine thread. It started out filling one's heart to the point of bursting, painfully large and seemingly all-powerful. But life went on, and time passed, distance grew, pain faded, grief became bearable.

She'd fought so hard to hold on to all of that, thinking that she was holding on to Mark, but Mark lived in heaven. He was happy there. She believed it with all her heart and soul. How could she begrudge him that? Even had she the ability to do so, how could she ask him to give up that for a life here with her and

Clark? Even a good life and all its attendant joys could not compare with the ecstasy of heaven.

Oh, how she had railed at the unfairness of his death. She had seen loving another man as a repudiation of her marriage to Mark, but she had been wrong about that. She and Mark had belonged together for the duration of his life, but evidently not for the duration of hers. What she couldn't seem to grasp, what she couldn't quite reconcile in her own mind, was the idea that God might actually have given her a new love in a dream.

"Dixie?"

Vonnie's voice penetrated her thoughts, bringing her back to the moment. "Sorry. What were you saying?"

Vonnie brushed Dixie's hair back from her face. "Are you okay?"

Dixie smiled and nodded. Decision settled over her. Without any inner debate or weighing of options, she knew what to do. She knew, too, that she would be opening a door on a whole new stage of her life, a new world, even. Gulping, she took a deep breath.

"Mom, I need to tell you a story. It started right after we put up the swing set in the backyard. With a dream."

They parted in tears. Dixie didn't know why, really, and neither, apparently, did Vonnie. It wasn't sadness or fear that brought the tears this time. It wasn't grief or anger or even relief. Dixie decided, later, sitting before the open Bible at the scarred table in her kitchen, that it was wonder, amazement.

"Do I believe God speaks to us on occasion in dreams?" Vonnie had said after hearing the whole tale. "How can I not now?"

"It doesn't mean I'm supposed to be with Joel," Dixie had cautioned.

But obviously he was meant to be some part of her life, their lives. She was glad of that. Joel Slade was a wonderful man, everything a woman could ask for, in fact, in whatever capacity she was blessed enough to have him—Christian brother, friend…husband, father to her children.

Oh, who was she kidding? She was nuts about the guy, and God knew she had tried not to be. But how could she not fall for him? With Joel, the world suddenly seemed like a bright place of infinite possibilities, not the sad, dark cave she'd been living in, where only the past and grief mattered. With Joel, she could be happy again. They could be happy again, all of them—she, Clark, Joel, Vonnie, Sam, even Bess.

Dixie beat back the giddy feeling that thinking of such a possibility suddenly evoked in her. She wasn't seventeen again, imagining her Prince Charming. She laughed at that. Who would imagine a blind Prince Charming? Suddenly, she couldn't imagine any other kind. Nevertheless, she told herself sternly, these things took time and a measured, adult response. They had no reason to rush, after all. They could see what developed, let things take a natural course. She imagined attending church and sitting casually next to Joel and his mother again. After a few weeks, surely one of them would suggest dinner afterward. There would be meetings in the park and long chats in the sunshine. Eventually she'd make a point of inviting Joel over to the house again.

She tried to think what dating would be like. It wasn't as if he would invite her out to a movie. A concert, maybe? Lectures at the university? He'd think of something and, knowing Joel, it would be something she'd never expect.

Okay, Lord, she thought, smiling. *I'm opening that door and trusting You to bring through it whatever You will.*

A dull *thunk* put that thought on hold. Instead, she left her chair and moved down the hall that flanked the living areas. She passed the large central bath and two bedrooms, including her own, approaching the door at the end of the hallway. Carefully, she eased the door open, expecting to catch Clark up and playing in his room. He'd protested when she'd tucked him in earlier, insisting that he wasn't tired, but she had seen the exhaustion in his eyes and knew that the sooner their routine was firmly reestablished after yesterday's misadventures, the better. And she was right. Clark slept the deep, deep slumber of the innocent. If he had so much as moved since she'd tucked him in, she couldn't tell it by the soft glow of the night-light next to his bed.

Pulling the door closed, she wandered back into the kitchen and dipped down toward the chair, but before her behind even met the seat, a series of rapid *thunks* had her bolting upright once again. Heart pounding, she strained her ears. The next *thunk-thunk-thunk* sent her toward the back door.

Reaching toward the phone on the wall, just in case, she flipped on the outside light. Dressed in jeans, boots, tan leather gloves and a T-shirt under a lightweight denim jacket, Joel dropped an armful of logs next to the garage. Going down on his haunches, he began straightening and stacking the firewood. Weak with relief, Dixie shook her head. She really had to get the man one of those talking watches. She flipped the dead bolt and opened the door, stepping out onto the narrow patio, her house shoes scuffing on the concrete.

"Hey, hon," he called. Pushing up to his full height and tugging off his work gloves, he turned to face her.

"Do you realize what time it is?" she asked, belting her robe closed over her soft, knit pajamas as she moved toward him.

"Yep. Do you realize that it's all pretty much the same to me?"

She laughed about that, actually laughed. "What am I going to do with you?"

"Well, now, I've been thinking about that," he said, "and in all fairness there are some things you need to consider."

"Such as?"

He whacked the gloves against his thigh. "For one thing, marrying me would eventually mean moving away from here, at least for a time."

"Marrying you," Dixie parroted. So much for taking their time!

"The law school is in Norman, Dixie. No getting around that," he went on smoothly, "so we'd have to move, at least for a few years."

She lifted a hand to cover her mouth, torn between laughter and a snort of disbelief. If she did either, though, he might think the worst, that she was rejecting him. And she didn't want him to think that. Gulping, she quite brilliantly managed to say, "I—I see."

"It's not really that far when you think about it, though," Joel stated, "and Sam's retired now. He and Vonnie can come and go as they please. They'll come see us. We'll come see them. They've been looking forward to traveling, too, you know."

"No, I—I didn't know."

"Oh. Well, I guess they didn't want you to think…"

"That they were hanging around here for me and Clark," Dixie finished for him. And she'd thought Joel was the blind one!

"Did I ever tell you," he said quickly, "that Sam sent me messages after I was wounded?"

"No."

Joel nodded. "Recorded messages. There's a Web site. Anyway, he found it, and he got on there and just talked to me. It meant the world to me. I promise, we'll stay in close contact with our folks. I will, I mean. Unless you…" He cleared his throat. "There's something else you better consider, too," he said very seriously. "It could be quite a few years before we, I, make any real money. My military pension will see us—that is, me—through school and help us…" he sighed "…get established, but it can take years to build a private practice."

"A private practice," she echoed, just so he'd know she was listening, even though her head was spinning like a top.

He grimaced. "Yeah, I'm determined to keep an open mind about that, but at this point I just don't see me as corporate counsel or working myself to the bone for some big firm. You need to know that up front."

"Ah. I, uh…I guess that's something we ought to be praying about then," she muttered.

He grinned wide enough to light up the night.

"What?" she asked, completely confused.

"You said 'we.' You said *we* ought to be praying about me going into private practice, and you're absolutely right about that."

Well, he started it, she thought crossly. The next moment, she bit back a spate of laughter. Of course, they were talking in terms of *we*. It had always been about *we,* even before they'd met! Good grief, how thick and stubborn could one woman be? She swallowed and searched for something calm and innocuous and reasonable to say. "It's, um, good to be right sometimes."

"It is. It really is," he agreed solemnly, stuffing the gloves into his hip pocket. "I, uh…" He inhaled deeply. "I've done a lot of research, and you should know that you'll lose some of the income you have now."

As if that mattered. Mark had purchased a modest life insurance policy when they'd learned that she was pregnant with Clark. Dixie had used it to retire the loan on her car and tucked the rest into a savings account. The mortgage insurance that they'd carried on their house had paid off their home. That had allowed her and Clark to manage on Mark's Social Security survivors' benefits, but the money really meant nothing to her. She was thankful that she could be home with her young son now, but she'd always assumed that at some point she'd go to work.

"Clark won't lose his," Joel was explaining, "but that should be put back for college or something. It's part of his father's legacy, after all. Of course, we'll want to find a way to try to match that for the other kids."

"The other kids," Dixie echoed, her heart suddenly pounding.

Joel folded his arms, his handsome face set in stern lines. Dixie smiled, imagining how many subordinates had gazed on that same expression.

"I really thought about this one," he said, "and there's just not much room for compromise here."

"Oh?" Unexpected excitement nearly choked her; her heart felt as if it might fly right out of her chest.

"Clark needs brothers and sisters," Joel argued, "and I want them."

She didn't even try to stop the tears that spilled from her eyes or quell the joy that filled her as she whispered, "I've thought about that myself lately."

He stilled. "Have you?"

She tossed her head in an attempt to dislodge the tendrils of hair that clung to her wet cheeks, and gulped down the tears clogging her throat. "Just how many do you want?"

"As many as we can reasonably manage. And you're crying again."

She laughed, wiping her cheeks on the sleeve of her robe. "You already know that I love you, don't you?"

He dropped his arms and bent forward, bracing his hands on his knees like a runner gasping to catch his breath, and bobbed his head. "Just like. You know. I love you."

Laughter and sobs poured out of her in equal measure. "I'm not sure I deserve this!"

He straightened abruptly. "Oh, yeah, you do. Me, too. But I don't think that's really the point."

"What is?" she croaked, mopping her face again.

"The plan. God's got a plan for us, Dixie. God's always got a plan."

She didn't doubt it. Now. She sauntered closer. "When did you get so smart?"

"Hmm, well, it started about the time I found myself living in a world of darkness. I had a dream, too, Dixie. All I could see was white light, nothing else, but I could hear my mom and both of my sisters talking. Nothing important. Just visiting. People were singing in the background, and there was organ music, like at church. And kids. I could hear them running and playing and laughing. Then there was this voice, not a spoken voice, you understand, just…I don't know how else to explain it, but it said, 'I am the Light of the world.' And it's true. Without that Light,

His light, nothing else matters. I started smartening up right about the time I figured that out."

"You had a dream," she whispered, awestruck.

Smiling, he crooked his finger, drawing her close enough to slip his arms about her. "I still do."

"Me, too," she confessed joyfully.

He pulled her against him. "I'll try to wait until you're comfortable with this, but I feel like I've lost so much time with you and Clark already."

She laughed, her delight spinning up, surely, all the way to heaven. She saw Mark's face, smiling, happy for her.

"What are you thinking?" her future husband asked softly.

She pulled his head down to hers, whispering, "I'm thinking, yes, I'll marry you."

The time for talk had passed. They'd both heard everything they needed. It was time for joining, and that was exactly what happened with the kiss they shared then. They became a couple in that moment, as bound in their hearts as they would soon be in the eyes of the world. In a most amazing fashion, God had given them each other. He had given them a future, and a dream that neither could make come true without the other. Which was just as it was meant to be, as it was *always* meant to be.

Epilogue

"She's all wrinkly," Clark said with the devastating honesty of a boy not quite three months shy of his fifth birthday.

Dixie smiled, too tired just then to chuckle as the other adults in the crowded hospital room did.

"That's good," Joel observed, holding Clark still with one hand as the boy knelt on the edge of the narrow hospital bed. Joel used the other hand to smooth Dixie's hair. He hadn't stopped touching her, in one way or another, since her labor had started fifteen hours earlier. "You were wrinkly, too, and look how good you turned out," he told Clark.

"My goodness, Dixie, she looks just like you," Vonnie said, and Bess concurred happily.

"Look, she's got that little peak in her hairline, and curls, too."

"Dark swirls all over her little head," Dixie clarified for her husband's sake.

"If she looks like her mom, then she's a real beauty," Joel said, bending down to kiss his wife's forehead. With baby Elise cradled in her arms, their little family was connected by touch.

"I dunno," Clark muttered doubtfully. "She's kinda red."

Joel ruffled Clark's curls. "You mean you're not still red? Last photo I saw of you, you were red as a beet."

"Da-a-d!"

"No, it's true."

"Tell him, Mom! I'm not red."

"He's perfect, just like his sister."

"Must be a newborn thing," Joel said, grinning.

"She'll be a pretty pink by morning," Sam said in a gravelly voice. He had teared up. Again. He'd cried at their modest wedding just over two years ago, and ever since he'd wept at every happy moment in their lives, of which there had been many. Sometimes he wept when he spoke of Mark, too, which, conversely, he did with great ease now. Everyone did. Joel insisted. He wanted Clark to grow up with full knowledge of both of his fathers.

"Speaking of pictures," Bess said, aiming her camera, "everyone smile."

Instantly, Dixie was swept back to another time. Her heart swelled with love and, yes, a bit of sadness still. She suspected that sadness would always be with her. Oddly, however, it made the everyday joy that much sweeter. Still, she was taking no chances this time. She reached up a hand and caught the sleeve of her husband's shirt, pulling him closer for the shot.

Bess snapped several photos of the happy family. "Oh," she crooned, "look at you. You're every mother's dream."

Joel beamed so widely Dixie marveled that his face didn't split.

Bess waved a hand. "Okay. Nana and Pop's turn."

They took a group photo, then Joel and Clark drew away so Sam and Vonnie could flank the bed. Bess happily snapped away as Vonnie promised to return the favor. Bess, after all, was part of the family, and in a very real way, this had all grown out of her dream. Plus, she had proved to be the very best of mothers-in-law.

Some time later, while Bess coached Joel through his first diaper change, Sam looking on as Clark made choking sounds and provided running commentary, Vonnie sat on the edge of Dixie's bed and took Dixie's hand in hers.

"Bess, Sam and I are going to go soon and take Clark with us so you and Joel can get to know your daughter in private, and rest."

Dixie smiled, weary but so very happy. "Thanks, Mom. Oh, and happy birthday."

Vonnie brought her cheek to the top of Dixie's head. "What a birthday gift!"

Joel looked up, not that he could see what he was doing to begin with, and grinned. "Yeah," he said. "How're you going to top this next year?"

"Twins," Bess suggested.

"Bite your tongue," Dixie scolded laughingly.

"This one's good for a lifetime!" Vonnie exclaimed. "Pity it didn't fall on Mother's Day again."

"No offense, Mom," Dixie said, smiling, "but I'm glad it didn't. This Mother's Day is too special to be shared with anyone's birthday. I can't tell you how I'm looking forward to it."

Sam blinked, looking slightly alarmed. "Does that mean you're going to try to make it to church? I mean, isn't it too soon?"

Dixie laughed, remembering a time when her father had badgered her about going to church on Mother's Day. How thankful she was that he had!

"That's between Dixie and the good Lord," Joel said complacently. "Elise and I will leave it to them." He got his hands under the freshly diapered baby's little rump and head and lifted her to his face, nuzzling her cheek. "Isn't that right, sugar lump?"

Sam looked as if he might cry again.

Dixie gazed up at her misty-eyed mother. "I wouldn't dream of missing it. Dreams, I have discovered, have a way of coming true."

"Oh, indeed they do," Joel said, unerringly placing the babe in the crook of Dixie's arm. "When they're part of God's plan, they always come true."

Yes, she thought, *just look at us.*

What more could anyone ask for than living proof?

* * * * *

Dear Reader,

As a young widow, I dreamed that a hickory tree fell on my toddler son's new swing set. A tall, dark-haired, bearded man rescued my son in that dream. Imagine my shock when that tree actually fell. It was nothing compared to my shock when I later met that man! Unnerved, I fell on my knees.

My anger after the death of my young husband had kept me away from the Lord for many months. Strangely, it was just after I confessed my sin of anger that I had the dream.

But what did it mean?

The man in my dream had no doubt. He actually asked me to marry him on our first date. I actually agreed! Thirty-three years ago.

God is so good!

God bless,

Arlene James

THE MOMMY WISH

Kathryn Springer

To every woman who was once a little girl who loved horses (you know who you are!)

Trust in the Lord and do good; dwell in the land and enjoy safe pasture. Delight yourself in the Lord and he will give you the desires of your heart.
—*Psalms* 37: 3, 4

Chapter One

"What do you mean there's a glitch? What kind of glitch? I'm supposed to sign the paperwork on Monday!"

Julia Windham rose to her feet so abruptly that the chair she'd been sitting on started to tip over. Her fingers curled around the wooden spindles—an attempt to steady not only the chair but the sudden, uneven skip of her heart.

"Please sit down, Julia. I'll try to explain what happened." The thread of tension in Lucy Robertson's cheerful, customer-friendly voice hinted that she wasn't looking forward to the task.

Julia's gaze shifted from the Realtor to the bay window over her kitchen sink instead. On the opposite side of the pasture, the moss-covered roof of a house peeked through the trees. And a ribbon of gray smoke unfurled from the top of the stone chimney.

She turned accusing eyes on the woman seated at the kitchen table. "Wait a minute. Are you telling me that the...*the glitch*...is there?"

In my house, she wanted to add.

The only thing that prevented her from saying the words out loud was the knowledge that the house didn't belong to her yet. But it would. By ten o'clock on Monday morning.

Glitch or no glitch.

When Lucy had called earlier that morning and asked if she could stop by for a few minutes, Julia had assumed it was to talk about the closing. She hadn't even thought it strange that the Realtor had chosen a Saturday morning to go over the final details. The town of Clear Springs, Wisconsin, was so small and full of down-home charm that it wasn't unusual for people to discuss business over a cup of coffee at the diner rather than in an office building.

That cozy, everyone-knows-your-name way of life was one of the reasons Julia chose to live outside the city limits.

She took a restless lap around the room while she waited for Lucy to deny it.

Except that Lucy *didn't* deny it.

"I know this is going to come as bit of a shock, Julia." The Realtor sighed. "When you and I spoke on the phone after the attorney called and said that I should list the Kramer property, I had to go out of town for a few days. I left my…ah, mother…in charge of things. I did mention that I'd hired her part-time, didn't I?"

Julia vaguely remembered that she had. But if she weren't mistaken, Lucy had also mentioned that although Irma Robertson had recently obtained her real-estate license, her duties would be limited to answering the phone and scheduling showings.

"I think so. But you told Irma that I had already made a verbal commitment to buy the property, didn't you?"

The twin spots of color that tinted Lucy's cheeks answered the question. "I was only going to be gone a few days. I didn't think it was necessary to tell her that you've always had a standing interest in the Kramer place."

"And now someone else is interested."

Unfortunately, Lucy didn't deny that, either.

"The day after I left, someone called and said he was looking for a house in the country. I hadn't even bothered to log the property into the computer, but when Mom was still on the phone with him, she spotted the notes I'd jotted down. She saw a new listing and a potential buyer and decided it was…"

"A chance to prove herself." Julia finished the sentence when Lucy's voice trailed off.

"No." The Realtor shifted uncomfortably. "Divine intervention."

"Divine intervention." Julia repeated the words in disbelief.

"You know Mom." Lucy's shoulders lifted in a helpless shrug. "She doesn't believe in coincidences."

Julia wanted to argue that from where she stood, the situation seemed more like a cosmic joke than divine intervention. Especially given the fact that she and God hadn't been on speaking terms for a long time.

She couldn't believe this was happening. When Lucy had called with the news that Zach Kramer's only surviving relative had finally decided to sell the house next door, she'd been thrilled.

And now some…outsider…wanted to buy it.

What Julia couldn't figure out was why.

The acreage itself wasn't anything to get excited about—a small notch of land near the creek that bordered Julia's property. Tangled skeins of wild grapevine wove through the branches of the oak trees that circled the unkempt yard. The changing seasons had gradually taken their toll on the clapboard farmhouse, whittling away at it until only a glimpse of its original charm remained.

Did the person interested in buying it want to turn the house into a weekend retreat? Or fix it up and resell it for a profit?

Neither possibility set well with Julia.

"The client drove up and took a look at it…." Lucy paused and a shiver of unease skated down Julia's spine.

Every time Lucy paused, the situation got more complicated. And Julia didn't need complicated.

"So Irma gave him permission to spend the night there?" she guessed. "Is that something you let prospective buyers do now? Try out the property before they buy it?"

"Prospective buyers, no." Lucy studied the lace tablecloth as if she'd never seen one before. "Buyers…yes. The paperwork was signed an hour before I got back into town late yesterday afternoon. The property officially belongs to a man named Nick Delaney now."

"Wind River Farm. Does our farm have a name, Dad? Can we give it one?"

Nick Delaney suppressed a smile as he turned down the paved driveway just beyond the weathered sign Beth had spotted. If he could only figure out a way to bottle and distribute his ten-year-old daughter's enthusiasm, he'd be a multimillionaire.

"I don't see why we can't. Although it's not really a farm."

"Not yet." Beth bounced on the seat, her lively gaze taking in the scenery around them. "But it will be."

"How about you and I move in first? Before we start collecting animals like Noah?"

"Or we could all move in at the same time."

"Come to think of it, the house does have a unique, *country* odor." Nick couldn't resist teasing her a little. "The animals should feel right at home in our living room."

"The house smells great." Beth smiled blissfully, as if she'd spent the night in a four-star hotel rather than a drafty farmhouse. "Everything is great. I can't wait for Granna Claire to see it. She's been praying that we would find just the right house. And we did."

Nick hoped his mother would feel the same way when she got her first glimpse of the place that Irma Robertson, the woman who had given them an official tour of the place, had cheerfully referred to as "a handyman's dream."

To most people, it probably looked more like a nightmare.

"Do you think Ms. Windham will like the brownies I made for her?"

Another bounce. Another question. He'd been peppered with them from the moment Beth poked her head out of the sleeping bag that morning. Only this time, Nick wasn't sure how to answer.

The garrulous Irma Robertson, who'd provided him with brief but thorough background information on most of the residents of Clear Springs, had become strangely evasive when Nick had inquired about their closest neighbor. The only thing she'd said was that Julia Windham lived alone and "kept to herself."

Nick filled in the blanks, understanding it to mean that the elderly woman preferred to be left alone. Unfortunately, it hadn't translated the same way to his outgoing daughter.

While Nick had spent the majority of the morning taking an inventory of the repairs the house would need, Beth had been busy, too.

She'd added a box of brownie mix to the cart when they'd made a quick trip to Clear Springs to pick up a few groceries the night before. And his daughter had quickly set him straight about who was going to reap the fruit of her labor. When he reached for the pan cooling on the scarred Formica counter, she had informed him the brownies were for Ms. Windham.

A "welcome to the neighborhood" gift.

Nick didn't want to point out that since they were the ones who were new to the neighborhood, it made more sense that *they* be on the receiving end of dessert.

But he'd given in, because generosity—like flossing—was another important quality that Claire Delaney had encouraged in her granddaughter. It was up to him to keep the torch lit.

As a single dad, Nick had come to rely on his mother's wisdom and experience. She'd braved the shopping malls for school clothes in the fall and organized Beth's annual birthday parties. Her sense of humor and deep faith had helped smooth out the rough spots after Liz died.

Nick had finally given up trying to repay his mother because he didn't think he could. The opportunity, however, had unexpectedly presented itself on Christmas Eve. A widower named Robert Owens had been visiting their church and happened to sit next to them during the fellowship time after services.

Nick figured it was the first time in Claire Delaney's life that she had deliberately ignored someone. Which told him more than anything how impressive the man had been to his mother.

It also gave him an opportunity to do what any good son would for the mother who had put her life on hold for eight years in order to make his a little easier.

He and Beth had invited Robert over for dinner.

Robert had accepted the invitation. And the next. In fact, the retired surgeon wisely had accepted every dinner invitation that followed until he'd won Claire over.

It hadn't taken long. A month ago, Nick had walked his mother down the aisle. Beth had been the maid of honor.

Before she had left for her honeymoon cruise, Mom had ambushed him, suggesting that maybe it was time for him to make a new start, too. At first, Nick had rejected the advice.

A new start? He was doing fine. He and Beth were both doing fine.

But she'd made him promise that he would pray about it.

In a roundabout way, the answer to that prayer was the reason he and Beth had ended up trading a two-bedroom condo in the Windy City for a fixer-upper that looked as if it belonged on the set of *Green Acres*.

"Look at her barn!" Beth squealed. "It's huge."

From the expression on his daughter's face, Nick could tell she was trying to determine just how many horses a barn that size could hold.

As they pulled up to the house, the curtains in the window drifted shut. It occurred to Nick that maybe it wasn't such a good idea to drop in unannounced on an elderly woman who lived alone on an isolated country road.

"Beth, why don't we—" *Come back another time,* he was going to say. After they'd called first.

"Get the brownies, Dad!" His daughter had unbuckled her seat belt and was already scrambling out of the car.

By the time Nick had closed the car door, Beth was halfway up the flagstone walkway that led to the front door.

Because it was tucked away in the sheltering circle of a stand of oak trees, Nick hadn't realized the house was so big.

Or so imposing.

His gaze moved from the stately two-story brick home to the L-shaped barn farther down the driveway. Several outbuildings fanned out around it, all of them painted an identical shade of brick-red and trimmed in white. Flower boxes lined the multipaned windows of an oversize shed, ready for spring planting.

There was an understated elegance to everything. In fact, it looked more like a country estate than a farmhouse. And it was a far cry from the house that he and Beth were going to call home.

Nick resisted the sudden urge to check for a servants' entrance at the back.

By the time he reached Beth's side, she'd enthusiastically tried out the bronze door-knocker several times.

She frowned up at him. "I don't think anyone's home."

"That's all right." Nick tried to hide his relief. It was probably better this way. "We can leave the brownies on the porch with a note."

"But her dog might eat them."

"I didn't see a dog."

"Neither did I, but she has to have one. It's a farm, Dad."

Nick knew there was no point in arguing. Beth firmly believed that everyone who lived in the country would have as many animals as possible. Just because they could.

"Fine. I'll find a safe place for them while you run back to the car and write Ms. Windham a note. There's paper in the glove compartment."

Beth looked disappointed but darted back to the car to carry out her part of the mission.

While Nick tried to decide the best place to keep the pan of brownies away from a dog that may or may not exist, the front door opened.

A woman stepped onto the porch but she wasn't the elderly neighbor Nick was expecting to see.

Not even close.

This woman was in her mid to late twenties. Tall and slender, her cap of honey-blond hair framed delicate features—sculpted cheekbones, a small, straight nose and a pair of stunning, violet-blue eyes.

Nick blinked.

Because the cool look in those stunning, violet-blue eyes made him sorry he *hadn't* checked for that servants' entrance.

"I'm… We're looking for Julia Windham. I'm Nick Delaney." He extended his hand. "My daughter, Beth, and I are moving into the house down the road. We wanted to stop by and introduce ourselves."

After a moment's hesitation, she touched her fingers to his in the barest of handshakes before quickly pulling her hand away.

"I'm Julia Windham."

Chapter Two

Nick Delaney.

Moving into the house down the road.

Julia barely had time to connect those two shocking pieces of information when the petite, redheaded whirlwind she'd seen from the window skidded up to them.

"I'm Beth Delaney." The girl grinned up at her. "We thought you'd be old. Dad and I were just about to leave the brownies on the porch. I didn't want to because I thought your dog might eat them. Chocolate isn't good for dogs, you know. Dad's a veterinarian so I know all kinds of things about animals…."

"Brownies?" Julia slipped in the question when Beth Delaney paused to take a breath. She was trying to make sense out of the "we thought you'd be old" comment when another one registered. "Dog? I don't have a dog."

Disappointment clouded Beth Delaney's big brown eyes for a moment. "Cats?" Her tone was hopeful.

"No. No cats, either." Julia fought the strangest urge to apologize.

"But you have horses, right? We saw the barn."

Julia sucked in a breath. Funny how one simple question possessed the power to pierce her defenses and scrape against a wound that had never completely healed.

She shook her head. "No horses."

"But this is a farm." Beth looked confused. "I saw the sign by the driveway. Wind River Farm. All farms have animals. Dad said I could name our farm…unless it has a name already. Do you know if it has a name?"

Julia took a step backward. Toward the safety of the house. She shouldn't have answered the door. When she'd heard the car pull up and saw the little girl jump out of the passenger side, Julia had assumed she was involved in some sort of school fundraiser.

If she'd had any inkling the vehicle belonged to her new neighbors, she would have followed her first instinct and ignored the enthusiastic pounding on the front door.

Julia stole a glance at the girl's father and then quickly looked away.

She'd thought the situation with the house was a major complication but Nick Delaney could very well fall under a whole separate category.

They had expected her to be old? Well, the Delaneys hadn't been the only ones guilty of making false assumptions.

Julia's imagination had created a picture of the man who had snapped up what was supposed to have been her land and it had been what the locals referred to as a "weekend warrior." A middle-aged man in Bermuda shorts and a polo shirt—holding a chain saw in one hand and a fishing pole in the other.

Nick Delaney, with his tousled sable-brown hair, jade-green eyes and ruggedly masculine features, fit the warrior part of the equation, at least.

That was what was so unsettling.

Not only did he possess traffic-stopping good looks but he also had the appealing aura of a man who didn't seem to *know* he possessed traffic-stopping good looks. If someone found that quality appealing. Which Julia didn't.

"Does our farm have a name?" Beth repeated the question, tilting her head in a curious way that reminded Julia of the chickadees that visited the bird feeder outside her kitchen window every morning.

"I don't think so," Julia murmured. "Everyone around here calls it the old Kramer place."

Beth's freckled nose pleated. "It's too pretty for that name. After Dad and I fix it up it'll look even better. We stayed there last night, and next Saturday we're going to bring the rest of our stuff."

"You're going to *live* there?" The words spilled out before Julia could stop them and her eyes flew to the girl's father. "I thought…when Lucy Robertson said you were from Chicago, I assumed you would be spending weekends there. Or maybe fixing it up in order to resell it."

"No—we're here for the long haul." Nick Delaney sounded way too cheerful about it. "I accepted a partnership with Dr. Blake."

"I see." Julia braced one hand against the doorjamb. She vaguely remembered hearing a rumor that Thomas Blake, the small-animal vet, was planning to retire soon, but most people had assumed his son would return to Clear Springs and take over his practice.

"The house needs a little bit of work but Tig and I are up to the challenge, aren't we?" Nick reached out and gave his daughter's copper ponytail an affectionate tug.

"Dad! I told you not to call me that anymore." Beth's slim shoulders rolled in time with a long-suffering sigh. She gave Julia an apologetic look. "Dad says I remind him of Tigger because I have a lot of energy. It's kind of a baby name, though, and I'll be eleven in a few weeks. I hope I get a puppy for my birthday."

Wonderful. Julia's lips tightened. With no fence between the two properties, the Delaneys' new pet would probably be a frequent visitor. Digging up her flower beds. Barking incessantly…

Her gaze suddenly collided with Nick Delaney's. His smile faded, the jade-green eyes darkening as if he'd read her thoughts.

Julia lifted her chin, forcing herself not to look away. This was her porch. She wasn't the…the interloper here.

"Beth, why don't you give Ms. Windham the brownies?" Nick suggested softly. "I think we've taken up enough of her time. And we should be back on the road before dark."

"Okay." Beth flashed a sunny smile as she retrieved the pan from the porch rail and proudly presented the foil-wrapped plate, crowned with a topknot of yellow curling ribbon.

She was about to reject his daughter's gift.

Nick's breath stalled as Julia Windham stared at the plate in Beth's hands as if she were being offered a dose of hemlock.

Take it. Please.

He didn't know how Beth would handle the rejection. His baby girl had a tendency to see the good in everything. And everyone.

He, on the other hand, should have seen this coming.

Julia Windham's chilly demeanor hadn't thawed a bit since she'd stepped onto the porch. The expression on her face sure hadn't matched the word *Welcome* stamped in gold letters on the mat beneath her expensive leather shoes. If anything, she had become even more reserved after Beth had quizzed her about the pets she owned.

Just what he needed. A neighbor who didn't like children or animals.

Until now, Nick hadn't realized how much he'd hoped that their "elderly neighbor" would become somewhat of a surrogate grandmother to Beth. Someone to fill the void of his mother's absence.

Okay, Lord. What's going on? Clear Springs is great. The job looks promising. The house is everything we wanted…but Julia Windham as a neighbor? Sorry—I must be missing something here.

What kind of person turned down chocolate? Handmade by a cute little redheaded kid?

Nick saw Beth's smile falter and his heart slammed against his rib cage. He took a step forward…

Just as Julia reached out and took the plate from her.

"I… Thank you." Her smile looked forced. "Did your mother help you make them?"

"Nope. It's just me and Dad," Beth said matter-of-factly. "Granna Claire taught me how to bake. She said it takes two people to make enough cookies to satisfy Dad's sweet tooth—"

"Beth." Nick saw his daughter's eyes widen and realized he'd spoken more sharply than he had intended. But he doubted Julia was interested in the mundane details of his personal life. "It's time to go. We've got a few more things to do before we leave." He gently put his hands on her shoulders and directed her toward the car.

"Let me know if you like the brownies!" Beth slipped from his grasp and Nick knew what was about to happen. Unfortunately, he wasn't fast enough to prevent it.

His daughter was a hugger. No one was exempt. It was a gene she'd inherited from her mother, so he'd indulged the habit.

Until now.

"Beth—" He swiped at her sleeve and ended up with a fistful of air instead.

Beth's arms clamped around Julia's slim waist. "Thanks for having us over. We'll stay longer next time. Promise."

Julia stiffened and Nick wasn't sure if she was going to scream or shake his daughter off like a piece of tissue paper stuck to the bottom of her shoe. Or both.

One hand came up and fluttered a few inches away from Beth's head. Oh, no. He hadn't thought of that one. Yanking his daughter's glossy ponytail would definitely lead to instant escape….

"Thank you." Julia gave her an awkward pat instead. Once. Twice.

Beth released her with a grin. "It was nice to meet you. Bye!"

With a quick nod, Julia dove for the door. It slammed shut behind her.

"Come on, Tig." He reeled Beth in and gave her the kind of hug she deserved.

On the drive back to Chicago, Nick had time to think about

Julia Windham. And the expression on her face before she'd disappeared into the house.

Given the woman's less-than-welcoming reception, he had expected to see displeasure. Or impatience. But oddly enough, the emotion that skimmed through those incredible violet eyes had looked more like...pain.

Chapter Three

"Go home, now. You aren't welcome here."

A pair of liquid-brown eyes stared sorrowfully at Julia over the heirloom rosebush she'd been trimming.

"I mean it." She sat back on her heels and frowned at the uninvited guest. "I don't have time for company."

Aahroorooroo!

Julia dropped the pruning shears and clamped her hands over her ears.

The newest addition to the neighborhood—Nick Delaney's enormous mongrel of a dog—mistook the shooing motion she'd made with her hands for an invitation to play. As if the animal were hinged in the middle, the front end of its body dropped to the ground while the part with the tail remained in the air.

Two furry eyebrows twitched hopefully.

"You couldn't have been a Chihuahua, could you? Oh, no. They had to adopt the biggest—" Julia stopped herself from saying the word *ugliest* only because the poor animal had had no choice about its questionable pedigree. One part timber wolf and two parts polar bear. "*Loudest* dog they could find."

Not to mention the smelliest.

The plumed tail slashed the air and Julia reared back.

Ach.

The creature was shedding so much fur it looked as if they'd experienced a mid-April snowfall. Julia picked a rogue hair off her sweater and flicked it away.

"Where is your family, by the way? Shouldn't they be keeping a closer eye on you?" Once again, Julia found her gaze drifting to the house across the field. Something that was happening way too often as the day wore on. But who could blame her? The quiet country road she lived on had become Grand Central Station over the past few hours.

The traffic had started just before noon, when Nick Delaney's car had chugged past—part of a caravan that included a moving truck and an apple-green SUV with the Robertson Realty logo on the side.

Julia guessed that Lucy had stopped by to officially present Nick with the keys to the house that should have belonged to her.

While the movers began unloading all of Nick and Beth Delaney's worldly possessions, Tom Blake's pickup had pulled up. That was when the dog had made its first appearance.

She had assumed—*hoped like crazy*—the shaggy monster tearing around the yard belonged to Dr. Blake. But when the vet finally drove away, the dog had stayed. He'd either left it behind on purpose—and Julia wouldn't have blamed him a bit—or else Nick Delaney had decided to present his daughter with an early birthday present.

As if on cue, a flash of yellow caught Julia's eye. A small figure shot out the back door and ran around the house. Seconds later, a shrill whistle rent the air.

"Beth is sounding the alarm." Julia arched a brow at the dog. "You better go home or you'll be in big trouble."

The animal grinned and rolled over, exposing its furry belly for a scratch.

"You are pitiful. You know that, don't you?" Julia reached for the heart-shaped tag dangling from a bright fluorescent-pink collar. "Belle. They named you Belle? As in beautiful?"

The bushy tail thumped an affirmative.

Julia gave in and rubbed her knuckles against the furry muzzle. The dog's tongue swiped her hand in appreciation.

"Okay, enough of that." Julia chuckled and rose to her feet. The muscles in her thigh contracted in protest. She stared across the field, absently kneading the familiar ache that bloomed in one hip. She looked down at the dog and sighed.

"If I want you to go home, then it looks like I'm going to have to take you there myself."

"I found Belle, Dad! She's with Julia."

"Ms. Windham," Nick corrected Beth while inwardly he stifled a groan. It was just his luck that the dog had decided to trot over and introduce herself to their neighbor.

He hadn't planned to adopt an animal the same day they moved in but a logging crew had found Belle running loose in the woods the day before, miles away from any homes or cabins. The closest animal shelter was an hour away, so Tom Blake had agreed to take her in temporarily. Nick had a hunch his new business partner had known that once a certain little redhead spotted the dog, it would have a permanent home.

His thoughtful boss had even thrown in a brand-new collar and a bag of dog chow.

Nick hadn't minded. One of the reasons he'd looked for a house in the country was so Beth could indulge her love for animals. Something their city apartment lease hadn't allowed.

He could only imagine what Julia would have to say about the first addition to his daughter's menagerie. On second thought, it looked as if he were going to find out. Whether he wanted to or not.

"I'll be there in a minute, sweetheart. Mrs. Robertson and I are almost finished here."

"I believe we are finished." In a sudden flurry of movement,

Lucy Robertson began to collect the paperwork. "You can call *me*—" Nick didn't miss the slight emphasis on the word "—if you have any questions."

Nick nodded, a little confused by the mixed signals he'd been getting from her. They'd started when he dropped by the realty agency and a subdued Irma Robertson had immediately summoned Lucy instead of dealing with his questions herself. The owner had seemed relaxed and friendly at the office but her attitude had changed the moment she'd arrived at the house. Lucy had been alternately fidgeting, tapping her pen against her teeth and sneaking little glances at the clock for the past half hour. Now she looked ready to bolt.

"I appreciate your taking the time to make a house call so I could be here to supervise the movers, Mrs. Robertson." Nick smiled. "And please tell Irma that I appreciate her willingness to show me the property last week on such short notice. I still can't believe the way everything worked out."

"Neither can I," Lucy muttered.

"Beth and I can't thank you enough for making this happen."

"Oh, please. Don't thank me." Lucy glanced out the window and her eyes widened. She began to inch her way toward the door.

"You'll call the Kramers' attorney when you get back to the office? To make sure everything is official?" Everything had happened so fast; Nick didn't want to take any chances. Not when Beth had already claimed the upstairs bedroom as her own.

Lucy's fingers closed around the handle of the screen door. "Of course, but I don't foresee a problem. Your bank called and everything appears to be in order. A second offer should no longer be an issue."

"Second offer?" Nick repeated. "Are you telling me that someone else put in an offer on the house?"

He half expected Lucy to deny it but she hesitated instead. "It's not unusual, you know." The unhappy look on her face told Nick that she regretted mentioning it. "If another buyer comes in and offers cash or has no contingencies, the seller can accept another offer instead...."

And bump the other one out.

Nick exhaled slowly.

The deal had been at risk and he hadn't even been aware of it. While he and Beth had spent the week making plans for their new home, someone had tried to take it away.

Thanks for looking out for us, God.

Nick scraped a hand across his jaw. "I hope the person interested in buying the property won't hold a grudge. I do have to make a living in this town, you know." He was only half joking.

Lucy didn't answer.

Not a good sign.

They heard voices outside and the Realtor paled. "I really should be getting back—"

The bottom dropped out of Nick's stomach as Lucy's peculiar behavior suddenly made sense.

"Julia Windham put the offer in, didn't she?"

Lucy made a strangled sound and her chin jerked once in affirmation.

"But she already has a...house." Nick stopped himself from saying the word *mansion*. "Why does she need another one?"

"It's not a question of need," Lucy explained in a low voice. "When Julia's grandfather was a young man, he deeded some land to his friend Zach Kramer as a gift. Julia isn't interested in the house. This little piece of land...your land...was part of Wind River Farm once. The Windhams have wanted to buy it back for years."

"So why didn't they buy it after Zach passed away?"

"Because he left it to his older brother—who everyone assumed would sell the place because he lives in California," Lucy explained, obviously warming to the subject even though her voice didn't break above a whisper. "For some reason, Bob Kramer refused. At first it might have been for sentimental reasons but later I think it was out of sheer stubbornness. From what I heard, Tara Windham, Julia's mother, had her attorney pestering him constantly."

"But it was Julia who put in the second offer. Hoping I'd have a contingency so she could bump me out." Unexpected disappointment crashed over Nick as the truth sank in.

He hadn't expected to join their new neighbor for evening sing-alongs by the campfire but he hadn't expected to get stabbed in the back, either.

Julia hadn't wasted any time trying to get her hands on the property. At least it explained the chilly reception he and Beth had received when they'd shown up on her doorstep.

Nick had been a little disturbed by how often he'd found himself thinking about Julia over the past week. He'd even convinced himself that she was shy rather than standoffish. Reserved rather than snobby.

Now he wondered if Julia had been eating one of the brownies Beth had made while she called the Realtor and tried to take their house away.

To his surprise, Lucy Robertson defended Julia. "If I had to guess, I'd say that Tara probably pressured Julia to put in the offer."

"I didn't meet anyone named Tara. Irma told me that Julia lived alone." That was why Nick had assumed she was a senior citizen.

You assumed a lot, didn't you, buddy?

"She does. Tara moved away shortly after the accident." Lucy's eyes clouded. "Such a tragedy. I'm afraid it changed her. People talked about it for months."

Nick frowned. "Julia's mother was in an accident?"

"No, not Tara. Julia."

Chapter Four

"Isn't Belle sweet, Ms. Windham?"

Julia winced as one of the dog's massive front paws crushed her toes.

Sweet? Not exactly the word *she* would have chosen.

"She's very…big."

Beth grinned. "Dr. Blake says she'll be a great watchdog."

Julia hid a smile of her own. She didn't doubt for an instant that the amiable giant would watch a burglar break into the house and help himself to the valuables inside.

"Dad's talking to Mrs. Robertson, and the movers are almost done. Do you want to see my room?"

Now that Julia had successfully reunited the dog with its owner, all she wanted to do was go home. And avoid seeing Nick Delaney again.

She still remembered seeing the confusion—followed by the flare of panic—in his eyes when she'd hesitated a split second too long before accepting Beth's gift. And if Nick had had an opportunity to talk to Lucy, he would understand the reason *behind* that hesitation….

"I don't think—"

"Great. Come on." Beth grabbed her hand and towed her across the muddy yard toward the back door.

Before Julia knew it, she was standing in the kitchen. Face-to-face with the very man she'd wanted to avoid. The abrupt silence that filled the room and the guilty look on Lucy's face told Julia exactly what the topic of their conversation had been.

Something she should have been used to by now.

"Yes, well…good luck settling in, Nick. Um, nice to see you again, Julia." The Realtor made a break for it and the screen door snapped shut behind her.

Julia forced herself to meet Nick's gaze, and her heart missed a beat.

Over the past week, she'd tried to convince herself that her memory had exaggerated how attractive he was. It hadn't. And that his eyes weren't really *that* green. They were. But when those eyes locked with hers over Beth's head, wariness replaced the friendly warmth Julia had seen in them the day they'd met.

What did you expect, she chided herself. *That Nick Delaney would be thrilled when he found out you wanted to take away his house?*

If only he understood the reason why.

It doesn't matter, does it? It isn't like you'll ever have an opportunity to explain it.

Beth skipped through the maze of cardboard boxes to her father's side. "Julia—I mean Ms. Windham—wants to see my room, Dad," she said cheerfully. "Is that okay?"

One of Nick's dark eyebrows shot up.

Julia's cheeks heated as she choked out a denial. "I didn't say that I…" She took a step backward and bumped into a furry wall. A rough, pink tongue swiped her hand.

Beth giggled. "See? Belle likes you."

"Great." Julia forced a smile as the dog collapsed at her feet.

Nick's lips twitched. "Thank you for bringing her home. She must have escaped when the movers left the door propped open."

Escape sounded good to Julia. Unfortunately, it wasn't an option with a furry chin propped on her shoe.

Beth darted back and tucked her arm through Julia's as if they'd known each other for years. Julia stiffened, not completely comfortable having her personal space invaded so easily. But something about Beth Delaney's sweet personality made it difficult to keep her usual boundaries in place.

"After you see my room, I'll show you the paint that Dad and I picked out," Beth said. "It's called 'rose petals.' Pink is my favorite, favorite—"

"Beth," Nick interrupted, his husky voice pleasant but firm. "We still have a lot of unpacking and I'm sure Ms. Windham has things to do, too. Maybe another time would be better."

He was offering her an out. One Julia should have been eager to accept…until she saw the disappointment on Beth's face.

"I suppose I have a minute."

Twenty minutes.

Nick paused at the bottom of the staircase. Judging from the trapped look in Julia's eyes, he had expected her to take a quick peek at Beth's bedroom and then hightail it back home.

Especially after the enlightening conversation he'd had with Lucy Robertson.

Nick shook his head, amazed at the way things had worked out. If even the smallest detail hadn't fallen into place, Julia would own the property and he and Beth would still be searching for a place to live. If Irma Robertson had told him about Julia's interest in the house, he would have backed off and looked for something else. But things hadn't happened that way and Nick recognized a gift when he was given one.

I see your hand in this situation, Lord, but I sure don't know what you've got planned. All I know is that Beth loves this place….

And he didn't want that to change.

Nick's fingers closed around the banister as a disturbing

thought pushed its way in. If Julia wanted the property so badly, would she happen to mention to Beth that it had once been part of Wind River Farm? That she'd always intended to buy it back if it came on the market?

Knowing his tenderhearted daughter, her joy would deflate like a day-old helium balloon if she thought they had taken something away—even accidentally—from someone else.

A cardboard box plastered with daisy stickers provided the perfect excuse to find out what was going on. Nick took the stairs two at a time and, as he reached the small landing at the top, he heard the sound of muffled voices coming from Beth's room.

"…this one is Gold Dust but I can't remember what kind of horse he is. It's kind of a weird name."

"A Norwegian Fjord," he heard Julia say. "You can tell by the short, two-toned mane."

Nick peeked through the gap in the door and almost dropped the box in his hands.

He'd put the bed frame together shortly after the movers had deposited it in Beth's room but planned to unpack the sheets and blankets later that day when he had more time.

Julia had beaten him to it.

He watched in disbelief as their new neighbor plumped up the pillows and smoothed out the wrinkles in Beth's favorite comforter. His daughter sat perched on a bright pink director's chair near the window, where the dusty ledge provided a temporary corral for her collection of model horses until Nick could put up some shelves.

Beth picked up another horse. "Granna Claire gave me this one for Christmas last year. She's on her honeymoon cruise right now but she promised to bring back a special one for my collection."

"Your…*grandmother*…is on a honeymoon cruise?"

"Yup. I was her maid of honor," Beth said matter-of-factly, as if there wasn't anything unusual or amazing about a grandmother going on a honeymoon cruise. Her voice lowered to a conspiratorial whisper. "Dad and I were the ones who got her and Grandpa Robert together."

"Really?" A soft, musical laugh followed the question.

Nick's heart reacted to the sound by trying to put a hole through his chest. And Nick reacted to that by almost dropping the box. Again.

"Yeah, but I miss her a lot. They won't be able to visit us for a while but Dad promised we can e-mail pictures of the house to them before I go to bed tonight. She's going to love it." Beth sounded absolutely certain. "We prayed that Dad and I would find the perfect house, and this is the one God gave us."

Nick closed his eyes briefly, uncertain how Julia would respond to that. His daughter may have been only ten years old but her simple, unwavering faith both humbled and amazed him. Along with her complete unselfconsciousness when it came to sharing it with others!

Through the gap in the door, Nick tried to see Julia's expression but her gaze remained riveted on the faded carpet, the silky tendrils of her tawny hair concealing her profile. But there was no mistaking the rigid set of her shoulders.

"Your dad is probably wondering what's taking us so long," Julia said quietly.

"Can't you stay a little longer?"

The plaintive question raised a warning flag in Nick's mind. Even though Beth was excited about the move, he knew she missed the girl talk that she and her grandmother had frequently indulged in. Something that he felt woefully ill-equipped to duplicate.

Nick was sure that Julia wouldn't be interested in serving as his mother's replacement. But in spite of that certainty, he couldn't help but be intrigued by the subtle contradictions he saw.

When Julia had brought Belle home, he'd braced himself for a lecture about unruly dogs and respecting property lines. Instead, she'd stunned him by giving in to Beth's plea to see her room and then listening patiently to the lengthy introduction—including names *and* breeds—of a herd of model horses.

A tragedy…it changed her. Not Julia's mother…Julia.

Fragments of his conversation with Lucy Robertson returned. She had mentioned something about Julia being in an accident but hadn't had a chance to elaborate.

But what kind of accident? There were no physical scars that he could see, but he knew from experience that some of the deepest wounds were on the inside. They were the easiest to conceal and yet they could be just as permanent. And damaging.

Nick couldn't shake the feeling there was more to Julia Windham than met the eye.

"I really do have to go," Julia said. "But thank you for showing me your room. And your horse collection."

Beth's face brightened. "Maybe Belle and I could visit you tomorrow after church. Do you go to Clear Springs Community? Dad and I are going to visit that one first because Irma Robertson invited us."

"I—"

Nick decided it was time to step in. Fast. He cleared his throat to warn them of his approach and then waited a second before shouldering the door open the rest of the way.

"Special delivery for a Bethany Claire Delaney."

"Look, Dad! Julia found all my blankets and made up the bed." Beth flopped across the mattress, hugging a daisy-shaped pillow to her chest.

"I see that. Thank you." Nick watched the color rise in Julia's cheeks before she averted her gaze.

"I prefer to keep busy," she murmured.

Why didn't he believe her? And why did she look embarrassed that he'd caught her doing something nice for Beth?

"Well, I appreciate—" *It.* Nick didn't get a chance to finish the sentence because Julia brushed past him and the faint scent of jasmine stirred the air, temporarily paralyzing his vocal cords.

Beth bounded after Julia, and Nick caught up with them at the bottom of the stairs to run interference. If he wasn't mistaken, Julia was about to be on the receiving end of another hug.

He tried to deflect it. "There's a surprise for you in the living room, Tig."

"Really? What is it?" Beth's excitement over the news spared him a scolding reminder that he wasn't supposed to call her by her nickname anymore.

"See for yourself."

Nick breathed a sigh of relief as Beth veered toward the living room, where he had spread out a checkered blanket in front of the fireplace.

"A picnic!" Beth dropped to her knees and admired the centerpiece—a jelly glass full of wild violets—that Nick had discovered growing along the foundation of the house. "This is so cool, Dad. What did you make?"

"A call to a local pizza place," Nick admitted. "I haven't unpacked the kitchen boxes yet."

Beth's smile widened to include Julia. "We're having a…what's it called again, Dad?"

Nick raked his fingers through his hair. Maybe it hadn't been such a good idea to surprise Beth with a picnic until *after* Julia had left.

"A housewarming party," he muttered.

"That's right. People have one of those when they buy a new house," Beth explained, as if Julia might not be familiar with the tradition. "Only it isn't going to seem like a party with only two people."

Nick didn't need a GPS to follow his pint-size extrovert's train of thought.

"Do you want to celebrate with us?" Beth asked Julia, looking at him to rally support for the idea. "Julia can stay, can't she, Dad? There will be enough pizza—"

A succession of cheerful blasts from a car horn drowned out

the rest of the words. Distracted from her closing argument, Beth raced to the window.

"It's Mrs. Robertson!"

Nick strode across the room. Sure enough. Irma Robertson hopped out of a bright yellow bus with the words *Clear Springs Community Church* painted on the side.

A bus filled with people.

"Wow." Beth blinked.

Nick thought that just about summed it up.

Out of the corner of his eye, he saw Julia pivot sharply and walk toward the door.

Beth spotted her, too, and her face fell. "Aren't you going to stay, Julia?"

Nick thought he saw a flicker of regret in Julia's eyes, but when their eyes met over Beth's head, the cool mask was back in place. "It looks like you'll have more than enough people to help you…celebrate your new house."

Chapter Five

"Julia knows a lot about horses, Dad."

"Really." Nick kept his tone neutral as he flipped back the blankets on Beth's bed.

"She knows what a Norwegian Fjord is. Isn't that awesome?"

Beth held up one of the model horses, just in case there might come a day when her father would have to identify a Norwegian Fjord, too.

Nick held back a sigh. Julia's name had come up frequently over the course of the day. Too frequently. For a woman who visibly stiffened whenever anyone got within three feet of her, their neighbor had made quite an impression on Beth.

That concerned him.

Clear Springs was a small town. Julia Windham most likely knew the people that Irma had brought with her the day before and yet she'd disappeared out the back door without saying hello to anyone. Nor had she offered to join the volunteer crew that had given up a Saturday to help him and Beth get settled in.

That told him more than anything how Julia felt about them moving next door.

"Into bed now. You've got a big day tomorrow." Nick did the

same thing he'd done every time Beth brought up Julia's name. He changed the subject. "Are you sure you don't want me to drive you to school in the morning?"

"I want to ride the bus." Beth wiggled underneath the comforter. "Didn't Julia do a great job making my bed?"

Lord, give me strength.

"I suppose."

"I wonder where she was when Belle and I went to visit her this afternoon."

"When you did what?" Nick choked out the question.

"Went to visit her. I told Julia we'd come over after church today and say hello." Beth's forehead pleated. "But she didn't answer the door when I knocked. Her car was there but maybe she didn't hear me."

Nick closed his eyes. His original plan—*not talking about Julia*—didn't seem to be working.

Why should it? a pesky voice in his head taunted. *Not thinking about her doesn't seem to be working, either.*

Nick pushed the thought away. This was about Beth, not him. And he didn't want his daughter's feelings to be hurt if Julia rebuffed her continued attempts to be friendly.

"Beth—"

"I think I know why God gave us this house, Dad." Beth's winsome smile surfaced and Nick couldn't help but smile back. Not only because it never failed to melt his heart but also because he welcomed the momentary reprieve.

"Why?" He tweaked one of her copper curls. "So you can finally have real animals instead of plastic ones?"

"Nope. For Julia."

"For *Julia?*"

"She's lonely."

"Lone—" The second syllable got stuck in Nick's throat. He tried again. "I don't think she's lonely, sweetheart."

"But she lives all by herself. She doesn't even have a dog."

That was probably because she didn't want one, Nick was tempted to say.

"Some people prefer to be alone. And we have to respect that."

"Okay." Beth closed her eyes.

Okay?

"You understand what I'm saying, right?" he pressed. "Julia could be the type of person who likes her privacy. That's the reason she lives in the country. Alone. Without a dog."

"I understand." Beth rolled over. "G'night, Dad. Love you."

Nick stared down at his daughter suspiciously.

Beth understood him…but did she *believe* him?

"Well?"

The imperious tone on the other end of the line made Julia wish she had checked her caller ID before answering the phone. Not that she would have ignored a call from her mother but at least she would have had a few seconds to prepare for it.

"Well, what?" *Nice try, Julia, but you're only delaying the inevitable.*

Her mother's impatient sigh sounded like a tire losing air. "Honestly, Julia, don't pretend you don't know what I'm talking about. Why do you think I called?"

I don't know, Mom. To have a real conversation with me instead of the usual five-minute duty call you make so you can tell your friends that we talk once a week?

Julia took a restless lap around the room and ended up in front of the window—the one that offered a sweeping view of her property and the house across the pasture—just in time to see a yellow school bus chugging down the road.

As the vehicle rumbled to a stop near the mailbox, Beth streaked out of the house with Belle close behind, playfully nipping at the pink backpack that bumped against her owner's heels.

Beth's first day at her new school.

Judging from the spring in her step, it didn't look as if she was nervous or scared but it couldn't be easy to switch schools at the end of a semester. Julia found herself hoping that Beth would make some friends right away. She remembered what it had felt like to be the "odd man out" on the playground.

Another familiar figure emerged from the house, causing Julia's breath to stick in her throat. It was Monday morning, but Nick, in faded jeans and a sweatshirt, didn't look as if he were dressed to go to the office.

Beth spun around before she clambered up the bus steps and it looked as if she paused to blow her father a kiss.

After the bus rolled around the corner, Nick remained in the driveway, staring at the empty road. Belle sat at his feet and let out a series of sharp little yips, as if demanding to know why her favorite person had disappeared.

Julia felt a tug on her heart. Because something in Nick's posture made her wonder if he wasn't thinking the same thing.

It's just me and Dad.

Beth's words scrolled through her memory. She'd talked with open affection about her Granna Claire but hadn't mentioned a mother....

"Julia! Are you still there?"

Julia cringed. "Yes, Mom. Still here."

"Then why didn't you answer my question?"

Because I wasn't listening?

Not that Julia was brave enough to admit it. "I'm sorry. I got distracted. I'm in my office."

Staring at my new neighbor.

She wasn't about to admit that, either.

"I asked if you'd offered to give Nick Delaney more than he paid for the place," Tara snapped. "He could find a nice house in Clear Springs. One that isn't about to fall down around his ears."

Julia thought that was a bit of an exaggeration. True, the outside needed a makeover, but the interior wasn't as bad as she'd imagined it would be. Nothing that some paint and new carpeting wouldn't cure.

"I don't think Nick is interested in selling." Julia watched him pick up a stick and throw it for Belle. He moved with the fluid grace of a natural athlete and she felt a strange flutter in her stomach.

"You don't think Nick is interested in selling," her mother repeated after a moment. "I can't believe you're giving up so easily. I'm disappointed in you, Julia."

Julia felt the sting of the words even though she wasn't surprised by them. After all, she'd been disappointing her mother for years.

We prayed that Dad and I would find the perfect house, and this is the one God gave us.

Unbidden, Beth's words came back to her.

The little girl might believe the house was an answer to prayer, but to Julia it represented one more thing God had taken away from her.

Somehow, that didn't surprise her, either.

Chapter Six

Not again.

Nick walked around the house and whistled for Belle, although he had a sinking feeling he knew exactly to where the dog had run off.

The same place she'd run off to three times that morning.

He cupped a hand over his brow to block out the sun and squinted in the direction of Julia's house. Just as he'd suspected, a large white object lay sprawled in front of the door like a furry welcome mat.

Except Nick was pretty certain the welcome didn't extend to the neighbor's dog. Ruefully, Nick admitted that it probably didn't extend to the neighbor, either.

He didn't want to tie up Belle or confine her to the house on a beautiful spring day, but keeping an eye on her was proving to be a challenge while he tackled some of the items on his lengthy to-do list.

Irma Robertson and the volunteers from Clear Springs Community Church had made a significant dent in that list but Nick was still glad he'd put off his official starting date at the vet clinic for a few days. It gave him a chance to start fixing up his fixer-upper.

He started out in the direction of Julia's house, praying she wouldn't step outside and catch Belle trespassing. Or him. So far, he'd managed to pull off three covert ops but the odds of completing another successful mission were getting slim.

He slipped under the fence, slunk along a hedge of boxwood and, as he got closer to the house, he cleared his throat to get the dog's attention. "Come on, girl. This isn't your house."

A carpet-square-size ear twitched, as if a pesky mosquito were buzzing around it.

Nick ran out of hedge and dove behind the nearest lilac bush. "I've got a nice, tasty biscuit on the counter with your name on it."

Belle's eyelids flickered.

Yes. The magic word.

"That's right. A biscuit," Nick whispered.

Wide awake now, the dog lifted her head and let out a happy woof.

Nick shot out from his hiding place. "No! No barking if you want a biscuit—"

So maybe the word wasn't magic. Because Belle rolled to her feet and tipped her nose to the sky. And Nick knew exactly what would happen next.

Aahrooorooroo!

He stumbled up the steps and made a grab for the pink collar. And somehow ended up on his back. With Belle on top of him.

"We've got to get home," he gasped, twisting to avoid the swipe of a tongue against his cheek.

Belle didn't budge, leaving Nick to conclude that she had a limited vocabulary. One that included the word *biscuit* but not the word *home*.

"Off you go. Before—"

Julia appeared.

But there she was, staring down at him as if he were a smear on a microscope slide. She somehow managed to look beautiful even upside down; prim and proper in a lightweight yellow sweater that reminded Nick of sunshine.

"Julia." Her name came out in a wheeze.

"Nick." Julia's smile came and went so quickly that Nick decided he must have imagined it. More than likely, the weight on his chest was cutting off oxygen to his brain.

Forget about it, Delaney. You aren't going to get out of this one with your dignity intact.

He tried anyway. "Nice—" *breathe* "—day isn't, it?"

Julia tilted her head and a lock of golden hair followed the movement, caressing the soft curve of her jaw. She clapped her hands twice—she didn't even have to *say* anything—and suddenly he was a free man.

"Thanks." Nick's fingers performed a brief, exploratory search for broken ribs as he staggered to his feet.

"You're welcome."

They stared at each other.

As if Belle had decided it was her responsibility to break the awkward silence that fell between the humans, she butted her massive head against Julia's leg. Julia caught her lower lip between her teeth and backed away.

Apparently both people *and* dogs were expected to keep their distance.

"Come on, Belle. Time to go home." No way was Nick going to say the word *biscuit* again.

Belle's gaze bounced between him and Julia, as if she were trying to make a decision. And then the dog—*his* dog—sat down. Next to Julia. The plumed tail thumped twice.

Nick interpreted that to mean "so there" in dog-speak.

"Belle. Home."

In response, Belle did a belly flop at Julia's feet, propped her chin on her paws and closed her eyes.

Nick silently added "build kennel" to his to-do list.

"I'm sorry—" He was unable to finish the sentence because he suddenly felt short of breath again. But this time he couldn't blame it on having the canine equivalent of an anvil sitting on his chest.

A smile tipped the corners of Julia's lips. A *real* smile. One that backlit the violet-blue eyes and revealed a captivating dimple in her left cheek.

The unexpected jolt that burned a path from Nick's heart to his toes left him shaken. After eight years, he'd come to accept that *those* kinds of feelings had gone dormant.

There'd been several women in his former congregation who'd subtly let him know they would be open to pursuing a serious relationship, but Nick had never been moved by their interest. Now just one smile from Julia Windham left him as tongue-tied as a junior-high kid with his first crush.

Twin spots of color tinted her cheeks and Nick realized he was still staring.

Say. Something.

"I guess Belle would rather stay here a little longer." Nick was even more stunned by the realization that he didn't blame the dog a bit. He was tempted to linger, too. Which was crazy, considering the fact that Julia didn't want him on her property. Or living in the house next door.

"Excuse me." Julia ducked her head but not before Nick caught a glimpse of another smile. "I'll let the two of you work this out while I check my mail."

She started down the steps and Belle rolled to her feet, attaching herself to Julia's side like a well-trained guide dog.

Building the dog kennel moved to the top of the list. "We'll, ah, walk with you. We're heading in that direction anyway." Nick tried to focus on something else so she wouldn't catch him staring. Again.

"It's hard to get used to the quiet," he said, lifting his face to the sun as they fell in step together down the driveway.

"Quiet?"

Nick chuckled at the astonishment in Julia's voice. He realized that the birds' lively chorus in the trees around them didn't exactly meet the definition. "Okay, it's hard to get used to the sounds of nature instead of sirens and traffic."

"Not everyone adjusts to country living."

"You did."

Julia's gaze remained fixed ahead of them. "Sometimes a person doesn't have a choice. Sometimes they have to…adjust. Whether they want to or not."

There was something in her voice that Nick couldn't quite identify. Resignation? Regret?

"Growing up, I was a frustrated city boy. I must have read *Hatchet* a dozen times and I remember driving my mother crazy every time she found me sleeping under my bed instead of on top of it." Nick smiled at the memory. "Beth takes after me, I suppose. Her mother's idea of roughing it was staying at a hotel without a concierge."

If Nick were honest with himself, it was one of the reasons he'd stayed in the city so long. Chicago had been the place where he and Liz had met and eventually married. The place he felt closest to her. Moving away would have felt as if he were severing another connection with her. So he'd stayed. Until his mother had challenged him to pray about his future, and the answer had ultimately led him to a dilapidated old farmhouse. A house that already felt like home.

"But…Beth's mother will visit here, won't she? She'll want to see Beth's room and meet Belle."

Nick sucked in a breath, reminding himself that Julia wouldn't know anything about his personal life.

"Liz—" it didn't hurt quite as much when he said her name anymore "—died when Beth was two years old."

Julia's mask slipped and her eyes filled with compassion. "I assumed…"

"That I was divorced," Nick finished. "Don't worry. It's an honest mistake. Not too many guys are widowers at the age of twenty-four."

He still couldn't believe eight years had gone by. Sometimes it seemed as if the accident had happened a few days ago…and other times it felt as if it were a lifetime ago.

"Liz had met some friends for lunch and was on her way home. A driver ran a red light at the intersection." A condensed version of a day that had come close to destroying the underpinnings of his life. And faith.

If Liz hadn't left Beth at his mother's, he would have lost them both.

"I'm sorry."

Nick had heard those formal little words spoken dozens of times from people who had inadvertently stumbled into a similar conversation. But the faint tremor in Julia's voice went beyond sympathy. It sounded like…understanding.

She'd lost someone, too.

Who?

As much as Nick wanted to know the answer to that question, he wasn't about to risk the fragile connection that had sprung up between them.

Lost in thought, he suddenly realized that Julia had stopped at the end of the driveway, where two silver mailboxes were fastened to a single post.

"I don't have to ask which mailbox belongs to you and which one is mine." Nick couldn't prevent the low rumble of laughter that escaped. "It looks like I'll have to add 'put up a new mailbox' to my list."

"After you paint Beth's room?"

Nick frowned. "How did you know I was painting her room?"

"You have…pink paint. On your cheek."

Of course he did. Because being turned into a throw rug by a Samoyed-shepherd mix hadn't been humiliating enough.

Nick performed an exploratory search along his jaw. "Did I get it?"

"No, it's right…here." At the feather-light touch of Julia's fingers against the side of his face, Nick felt another breaker switch in his heart flip on.

Julia yanked her hand away and her eyes darkened with confusion.

That makes two of us, Nick thought.

He forced a rueful smile, sensing that Julia was ready to bolt. "Beth's favorite, favorite color."

"Rose petals."

Nick was surprised she'd remembered. "I guess it's a good thing she didn't insist on painting the outside of the house that color."

"You're painting the house?"

"Weren't you going to?" Nick asked without thinking.

A pause. And then, "I was going to have it taken down."

"Taken…" Nick's voice trailed off when the meaning sank in. "As in, demolished?"

"That's right." Julia's gaze shifted to the house. *His* house. "It's old and falling apart. It's an eyesore."

Why did he get the feeling she was repeating someone else's words?

"I guess that depends on whose eyes are looking at it," Nick said softly.

Julia didn't reply as she pulled a stack of envelopes out of her mailbox.

"I'm sorry about Belle," he said, reluctant to leave things between them on a bad note. "Beth and I will work on training her to stay in the yard."

Julia's hand kneaded the soft curve of her hip. "Thank you," she said, her tone once again polite. Distant. "I work out of my home so my hours vary every day. It's difficult to get anything accomplished if there are constant…distractions."

Nick read between the lines. Distractions like a precocious ten-year-old and her ninety-pound canine sidekick.

He tamped down the disappointment that stirred inside of him. With a little creativity, Nick knew he could keep the ninety-pound sidekick out of Julia's hair—and her yard. But he had a feeling the precocious ten-year-old would prove to be the greater challenge.

Chapter Seven

Julia's cell phone came to life in her jacket pocket, belting out the theme song from one of her favorite musicals.

"Hello?"

"Julia?"

At the sound of Nick's voice, the wooden spoon she'd been using to stir a batch of homemade spaghetti sauce slipped out of her hand and clattered across the kitchen floor.

"I'm sorry. Did I catch you in the middle of something?"

Just thinking about you was the first thought that popped into Julia's head.

"N-no." Her hands trembled as she bent to retrieve the spoon.

"I hate to bother you." Nick's ragged exhale on the other end of the line had Julia's fingers tightening around the phone.

"Is everything all right? Is it Beth?" The questions tumbled over each other.

"She's the reason I'm calling," Nick admitted. "I'm on my way to a house call. A dog was struck by a car and its owner is an elderly woman who lives alone. I usually pick Beth up after school and she stays at the clinic with me until we close for the day...." His voice trailed off and Julia connected the dots.

He needed her help.

"What about Irma Robertson? Or Lucy?" she blurted.

"Oh." There was a pause and Julia's could almost *see* Nick run his fingers through his hair. It was a little unsettling to discover that she was already familiar with some of his mannerisms. "I thought of you first."

Strangely enough, a feeling of warmth, rather than panic, bloomed inside of her at the admission.

"Beth needs a ride home from school?"

"No, I called the principal and Beth can take the bus home today. It's just that I'm not comfortable with her being alone, especially when I don't know how long this will take. I should have asked Irma. You're probably busy."

Not to mention she'd more or less told Nick that she preferred to be left alone. They both knew it—although he was too polite to remind her of their last conversation. The conversation that had plagued her with guilt—and regret—ever since.

It had been an evasive maneuver. A futile attempt to override the urge to comfort him when he'd told her that his wife had died. To tell him that she understood grief. And loss.

The troubling part was that even though she hadn't said a word, Nick had still known. She'd heard it in his voice. Seen it in his eyes. The fact that he'd looked past her defenses and discovered the truth had stirred up her flight response.

When she'd told Nick that she didn't need any unnecessary distractions, he'd thought she meant Beth and the dog. But the truth was, she found Nick a distraction, too. His appealing, lopsided smile. The husky, masculine laugh that wove its way through the frozen terrain of her heart, melting a path through her defenses like a warm spring breeze.

If she weren't careful, it would be all too easy to let Nick and Beth Delaney into her life. In less than a week, they already occupied more of her thoughts than they should. Beth's sweet personality and impulsive hugs made Julia long for things she could never have. And Nick…

She refused to let her thoughts go there.

Julia tried to come up with an excuse. A valid reason why having Beth over wouldn't work out. But she couldn't think of a single one.

"I'm not busy," she heard herself say instead. "Beth can stay here until you get home."

Silence. And then, "Great. I'll be there as soon as I can." The relief in his voice was palpable.

"Don't worry. She'll be fine."

"Oh, I'm not worried about Beth." Nick chuckled. "I know she'll be in good hands. I'm just sorry I had to inconvenience you."

"It's not an inconvenience." As soon as she said the words, Julia realized they were true. She didn't know what Nick had said to Beth, but neither the little girl nor her dog had made any impromptu visits over the past few days. Even though she tried to convince herself it was what she'd wanted, she couldn't help but feel a little…disappointed.

"Great. I'll see you soon."

Julia hung up the phone and glanced at the clock. In half an hour, Beth would be getting off the bus.

Panic squeezed the air from her lungs.

Was she supposed to fix her an after-school snack? Did she have anything in the cupboard that would appeal to a ten-year-old? Should she help with homework?

I know she'll be in good hands.

Nick's words scrolled through her mind, easing her momentary panic. He'd sounded so…confident.

Why did he trust her?

She'd been less than neighborly since they'd moved in next door. Rebuffed Beth's invitation to share a picnic lunch. She'd even put in a generous offer on the house that Beth believed God had provided for them.

Julia had tried to keep a safe distance…but the feelings that Nick stirred inside of her felt anything but safe. Watching him and Beth interact—seeing the affection between them—made her long for things beyond her reach. Things she'd accepted would never be part of her life. A close, loving family. A home filled with laughter.

In a single moment, those dreams had shattered along with the bones in her body. For a little while, her fiancé had held her hand and made her believe that everything would be all right. But in the end, Steve had walked away, too.

There was no point in dreaming. Dreams only led to disappointment.

Quarter to ten.

Nick winced, mentally practicing the apology he owed Julia.

He'd kept his promise—to get home as soon as he could. The trouble was, this was the soonest he could get home. Which meant Julia had been in charge of homework, supper and the general all-around mayhem that typically accompanied Beth's bedtime routine.

Maybe he should have stopped at the grocery store and bought a box of chocolates. To go along with the apology.

Maybe you shouldn't have called her in the first place.

Why had he? A split second after Julia had answered the phone, Nick had wondered why she'd been the first person who had come to mind when he'd been called out on an emergency. After stumbling through the explanation as to *why* he'd called, he half expected she would laugh. Or hang up on him.

He'd almost dropped the phone when she'd agreed to keep an eye on Beth until he could get home. And he hadn't imagined the undercurrent of concern in her voice when she'd asked if everything was all right. As if she actually cared that everything was all right.

But that didn't make sense, either, considering she'd all but told him that she wanted to be left alone.

He'd done his best over the past few days to keep his determined offspring so busy that she didn't have time to slip under the fence and drop by their neighbor's house for a visit.

He'd hinted that Julia worked out of her home...*no, he had no idea what she did*...that she wasn't too keen on being disrupted...*yes, it was possible Belle fell into that category*...and that it was important to respect people's wishes. And their privacy.

Beth had accepted everything he'd said but that didn't stop her from talking about Julia. Every chance she got. Or adding her name to the list of people Beth prayed for at bedtime.

God, thank You that we moved here.

The first time Nick heard that one, it was all he could do to stifle a groan. If Julia talked with God at all, he doubted she was saying a similar prayer.

Still, there were moments when she seemed to soften; making him wonder if some lingering pain below the surface had forged the cool reserve she used like a shield.

He thought about the smile she hadn't been able to suppress when Belle had plopped at her feet that day. The smile that continued to linger at the edges of his memory...

You keep lecturing Beth on keeping your distance. You should probably take your own advice, Nick chided himself.

As he guided the car around the corner, his foot came down hard on the brake. Julia's house was completely dark except for a soft glow in the kitchen window. His house, on the other hand, was lit up like a Christmas float.

It occurred to him that they'd probably switched houses because it was getting close to the time Beth went to bed and Julia didn't know when he'd be home.

Because my cell phone battery died. And Mrs. Vanderbeek's dog needed emergency surgery....

He parked the car and slipped inside the house, half expecting to find Julia waiting for him on the other side of the door. Tapping her foot.

The front hall was empty. There was no sign of Belle, who usually greeted him the moment she heard his key turn in the lock. Everything was quiet. So quiet that Nick wondered if he *had* gone to wrong house by mistake.

He made a quick search of the first floor and then padded up the stairs. When he reached the top step, he saw a sliver of light underneath Beth's bedroom door. Nick tapped on it before turning the knob.

"Anybody in here?" He pushed it open, his heart fisting at the sight that greeted him.

His daughter was already in her favorite pajamas and tucked under the covers. Propped up on her knees was the book of family devotions they read together every night.

That part of the scene, however, was a familiar one to Nick. The one that stole his breath from his lungs was the fact that she was leaning against Julia, their heads close together. Julia's long legs were tucked underneath her and a necklace made of braided ribbon and gaudy beads adorned the powder-blue cashmere sweater she wore.

In spite of the differences in their coloring, she and Beth looked as if they fit together like the last two pieces of a puzzle.

Nick felt the world suddenly shift beneath his feet. Swamped by an unexpected wave of emotion, he struggled to regain his equilibrium.

For eight years, he'd done everything he could to make sure that Beth didn't feel the void that Liz's death had created in their family. His mother had provided a wonderful role model. He'd made sure Beth had regular playdates with friends. He encouraged her interests and hobbies.

Nick had convinced himself that his daughter had everything she needed. Their lives were full. Their family complete, even though it was only the two of them.

What he hadn't realized until this moment was that he'd tried to convince himself of that, too.

The thought slammed against his defenses. Defenses that Nick hadn't even known existed. Until now.

For years he'd refused to date, telling himself that he needed to protect Beth from the complications a serious relationship would inevitably bring. But now, as if God were aiming a light into a shadowy corner of his soul, Nick realized that maybe, just maybe, Beth's heart hadn't been the only one he'd been protecting.

Chapter Eight

"Are you okay, Dad?"

Something must have shown on his face because Beth's eyes rounded in alarm.

Nick wasn't sure how to answer that particular question. So he avoided it by asking one of his own. "How did everything go?"

Beth grinned. "Good. We finished reading today's devotion and we were just about to pray."

Daily devotional readings. Prayer. They were an everyday benediction in the Delaney household, but what had Julia thought about the unexpected additions to her responsibilities? Which reminded Nick how late it was. How late *he* was.

He dared a quick look in Julia's direction. "I'm sorry you had to bring Beth back here for bedtime."

"We never went to my house. We decided it would be easier to stay here." Nothing in Julia's expression gave Nick a clue how she felt about the change in venue. Or anything else, for that matter.

Beth nodded vigorously. "We took Belle for a walk. And I had to feed the rabbits and put fresh bedding in their hutch."

Nick had forgotten about the rabbits. They'd recently adopted Sam and Walter from the second-grade teacher, who had come to the conclusion that twenty-four students and two bunnies was not a good ratio.

"Did you finish your homework?"

"I didn't have any tonight." Beth shrugged and caught the devotional book as it started to slide off her knees.

Nick's vision of Beth spending the evening engrossed in her homework while Julia went about her own business dissolved as swiftly as the apology he'd rehearsed on the way home. "What did you do?" He was almost afraid to ask.

"After supper we made chocolate-chip cookies for your lunch and Julia put up the curtains in my room." Beth's expression brightened. "Oh, we talked to Gran, too."

His mother had called?

Wait a second. Had Beth just said, "*We* talked to Gran"?

"She said she'll call again when they reach the next port," Julia said briskly as she slid off the bed.

Right. If Nick knew his mother, she'd be calling a lot sooner than that.

Julia looked poised for flight but Nick stood between her and the door. "Thank you again for keeping an eye on Beth."

"And Belle and Sam and Walter," his daughter chimed in.

Nick winced. There should have been an apology, chocolate *and* flowers.

"Thank you for taking care of…everyone," he amended.

"We had fun, didn't we, Julia?" Beth gave a contented sigh.

"Yes, we did." The flicker of vulnerability in Julia's eyes tugged at Nick's heart. As if she had surprised herself by admitting it.

"Night. You can keep the necklace…." Beth's words dissolved into a yawn.

Julia glanced down, as if she'd forgotten that a colorful garland of ribbon circled her neck. For a split second, the elusive dimple surfaced. "Thank you."

"I'll give you a ride home." Now that Nick thought about it, he hadn't noticed her car parked by the house.

"I don't mind walking." Julia politely but firmly rejected his offer. "I can cut across the pasture."

"It's no…" *Trouble.*

Nick found himself talking to empty air.

He caught up to her at the door.

"I really don't mind walking." Julia refused to look at him. *Couldn't* look at him. "It's a beautiful night."

"You're right about that." Nick's shoulders lifted in an easy shrug as he fell in step beside her. "Which is exactly why I don't mind walking you home."

"Beth—"

"Is watching us from the bedroom window. She and Belle will be fine for a few minutes."

Julia was glad the shadows concealed her panic. She didn't want to be anywhere near Nick Delaney. All she wanted to do was put the evening behind her and go home.…

Liar.

She stumbled a little, as if the truth had knocked her off balance. Because the truth wasn't that she wanted to go home. She'd wanted to stay.

An evening with Beth had given Julia a bittersweet glimpse of the kind of life she'd stopped dreaming about a long time ago.

They had done all the things Beth had told her father about, and a few more besides. The only awkward moment was when Granna Claire had asked to speak with her. Julia had reluctantly taken the phone from Beth, certain she'd be subjected to an interrogation.

Instead, Claire had expressed her gratitude that Julia had come to her son's rescue.

"I'm so thankful they have a neighbor like you," Claire had gushed. *"I have to admit I've struggled with guilt over being so far away but it helps to be reminded that God is looking out for them. I hope I get a chance to meet you when Robert and I come for a visit."*

Julia had squirmed under the praise. She had no doubt that if Nick's mother knew what had transpired with the house, she wouldn't be so quick to believe Julia was an answer to her prayers.

She wasn't an answer to anyone's prayers.

Especially someone like Nick. Not only was he incredibly attractive on the outside, Julia was discovering that his insides were just as appealing. He was a devoted family man. A man who opened his home to a growing menagerie of animals. A man who would eventually remarry and fill the house with brothers and sisters for Beth....

This time, the pain surging through her had nothing to do with the tiny spasms that shot up her leg as Julia quickened her pace.

"Hey, slow down." The husky amusement in Nick's voice rubbed against her already raw defenses. "Are you training for a marathon or something?"

The irony of the "or something" made Julia wince. Afraid he would see her expression, she stopped at the edge of the yard, where the moonlight merged with the shadows. "You don't have to go any farther. Beth will be waiting up for you and it's getting late."

Nick's chiseled features were washed in silver, his jade eyes searching as he stared down at her. For one heart-stopping moment, Julia thought he would insist.

"All right." She breathed a sigh of relief when he gave in. "Listen, I really do appreciate you putting aside your plans tonight to watch Beth."

Plans?

If the idea hadn't been so laughable, Julia might have smiled. Her plans for the evening had included cleaning out one of the outbuildings and then curling up on the sofa with the book she'd been reading. Nothing that couldn't be put off until the following day. Or the next.

A week ago, if anyone had asked, she would have insisted she was content with her solitary life. The life she'd chosen. But a few hours in the Delaney household had made that life seem boring. Empty.

There's no place for you there, she reminded herself ruthlessly as she pivoted away from Nick.

"What can I do to thank you?" Nick called after her. "I grill a great steak. And I've been told I make a mean hot fudge sundae, too."

More time spent in his company. Another evening being reminded of what she couldn't have. So why did a wave of longing rush through her? It took all Julia's will to keep walking, her frayed emotions unraveling with each step she took away from him.

"If you won't tell me, then I'll just have to think of something," Nick called after her.

Julia knew she should turn around and tell him that he didn't have to do anything. But she didn't. She found herself smiling instead.

And that was what frightened her the most.

Chapter Nine

"Julia helped me make necklaces for all the horses," Beth said between bites of pancake. "And she held Walter and Sam while I cleaned out their cage."

Okay. Nick *really* had to find a way to make it up to her.

The trouble was, every time Beth said Julia's name—and so far their entire breakfast conversation had revolved around the evening she and Beth had spent together—Nick swore he heard the sound of yet another wall crumbling around his heart.

He'd lain awake half the night, asking God why Julia Windham was the one who'd managed, in the brief time he'd known her, to resurrect feelings he'd thought had died with Liz.

"More pancakes?" Nick tried to distract Beth from any more talk about their next-door neighbor.

"Nope." Beth swallowed the last of her orange juice. "Julia said—"

"The bus will be here in a few minutes, Tig."

Beth rolled her eyes. "I'll be eleven on Friday, Dad. Remember?"

Nick smiled. How could he forget, when she reminded him at least twice a day? At least he'd hit upon a topic guaranteed to turn Beth's attention away from Julia.

"Have you decided how we should celebrate your birthday?"

"Can Julia come over and have cake with us? You said I could invite some friends over."

Give me patience, Lord. Right now would be great. "I meant friends from school."

"I don't have any friends yet."

"No friends?" Nick raised an eyebrow. Both the principal and Beth's teachers had assured him that she'd adjusted well to her new school and was popular with her classmates.

"Maybe a few." Beth stirred a pool of maple syrup around with her fork. "But it's tough being the new kid." Sorrowful eyes peered up at him.

Nick was tempted to ask if the school had a drama club she could join.

"Julia might have other plans," he said carefully. "Remember what we talked about—"

"Bus is coming!" Beth dove for the pink backpack at her feet. "Gotta go. Love ya, Dad!" She paused when she reached the door and tossed a smile over her shoulder. "By the way, Julia doesn't have a boyfriend. I asked her."

The door snapped shut but Nick's lower jaw was still hanging open.

A few seconds later, his cell rang, jarring him out of the near-catatonic state that Beth's parting words had put him in.

"Nick—I was hoping I'd catch you before you left for work."

He knew it. "Hi, Mom. You weren't supposed to call until the weekend. Is everything all right?"

"That's my line." Claire chuckled. "You sound a little dazed."

That about summed it up, Nick thought. "Just trying to figure something—" *someone* "—out."

"Beth."

"Bingo." Nick decided it was best not to mention the other woman in his life he couldn't figure out. Whoa. Wait a second. There *was* no other woman in his life. "I'm not sure what to do with her."

"What's going on?"

"She's getting a little attached to our new neighbor." And there, Nick thought with a shake of his head, was the perfect example of the pot calling the kettle black.

"Ah, Julia Windham." Was it his imagination, or did his mother sound a bit smug? "She seems like a very nice young woman. What's the problem?"

So Nick told her. Everything. How Julia had planned to buy the property. Her assertion that she didn't need distractions, then not hesitating to give up an evening to keep an eye on Beth. About Beth's insistence that Julia was lonely.

When he finished, there was absolute silence on the other end of the line. Nick waited. His mother not only knew her granddaughter well but she practically oozed wisdom. He was confident she could shed some light on the situation.

"Oh."

"Oh?" Nick repeated the word in disbelief. "That's it? That's all you've got?"

"I..." Claire hesitated. "I think I might know why Beth is so determined to befriend Julia."

Relief poured through Nick. "Great."

"You might not think so when you hear my theory," she murmured. "Normally, I wouldn't share a confidence, but in this case I should probably make an exception. Beth told you about her special prayer—"

"For the house."

"Yes. That was one of them."

"One of them? There's more than one?"

A sigh unfurled on the other end of the line. "You know Beth keeps a list of the things she prays for in her diary. Before Robert and I left on our honeymoon, she shared her top three with me. A house in the country..."

Nick waited. And waited. "Mom, I'm a big boy, remember? Let's hear number two."

"A horse."

Nick relaxed a little. So far, no surprises. Beth's love for that particular animal was no secret. "I know all about that one, too."

"Yes, well…"

"Come on, Mom. Give it to me straight," Nick teased. "I think I can take—"

"Beth has been asking God for a mother."

"What?"

"That's not all."

How, Nick wondered in disbelief, could there possibly be more?

"I have a feeling she thinks that God took care of two requests at the same time."

"Two requests?"

"Look at it from her perspective," Claire said, and for the first time Nick heard an undercurrent of amusement in her voice. "God provided the house in the country…and Julia, an attractive, young—and I might add, conveniently single—woman who happens to live right next door."

Julia retreated to the woods right after breakfast to clear her head. And to escape the verse she'd read in Beth's devotional book the night before.

It didn't work. If anything, it seemed as if everything around her kept repeating the words like a chorus. The breeze that whispered through the hardwoods. The birds singing in the branches above her head.

Trust in the Lord and do good…dwell in the land and enjoy safe pasture. Delight yourself in the Lord and He will give you the desires of your heart.

Had she ever truly trusted Him?

At one point in her life, she would have said she did.

But then, Julia thought bitterly, she also would have claimed she had everything her heart desired.

As the only child of the wealthiest family in the area, Julia grew up believing that Wind River Farm was the equivalent of a tiny kingdom. And from the moment Julia had been placed on the back of a horse at the age of four, she'd been expected to carry on the legacy that her mother, a former superstar in eventing competitions, had begun.

To a girl whose baby book claimed that one of her first words was "horsey," the hours she'd spent caring for the horses and taking riding lessons had never seemed like a burden. Julia preferred spending time in the barn to hanging out with her classmates, who mistook her shyness for arrogance. Not only that, but the barn offered a refuge when her parents' arguing escalated to the point that her father had walked out the door one day and never come back.

After he left, Tara had pushed her even harder. As trophies began to line the mantel, life became more about the exacting requirements of the ring and less about the simple pleasures Julia had found in a leisurely ride along the river. It hadn't taken long for her to realize that a judge's approval rating earned approval in her mother's eyes—something she longed for more than another ribbon or trophy.

Julia continued to meet every challenge, and her fearless confidence both in and out of the ring cemented her reputation as the golden girl of the horse show circuit. The reigning princess from Wind River Farm.

And then she'd met her prince.

Julia closed her eyes but it didn't prevent an image of Steve Ballad's handsome face from invading her memories. Their paths had crossed at a weekend cross-country event and, although Julia had beaten him, he'd asked her to dinner. Three months later, he'd proposed.

She'd had everything. Until the accident.

Julia had returned to Wind River Farm, not at the top of the world but in pieces at the bottom of it. Everything had changed. Tara had accepted a position teaching at a prestigious riding academy in Kentucky and Steve had broken off their engagement.

But her fiancé wasn't all she'd lost.

Julia sank against a tree.

When Beth had read the words in the devotional book the night before, a surge of longing had swept through her. And Julia knew why. She was tired of going through the motions of each day, alive but not really living. To anyone watching, she appeared to have everything together. Only Julia knew the truth. The injuries may have healed but the wounds on her heart hadn't.

Trust in the Lord…trust in the Lord.

Could she?

Julia closed her eyes and her heart formed the words before her mind could shut them down.

Please tell me that You're here, God. And that You care about me.

When she opened them again, she could see the faint outline of Nick's house beyond the trees.

Nick's house.

A smile curved her lips.

When had she stopped thinking of it as the old Kramer place?

When had she'd stopped thinking of it as hers?

Maybe when she'd realized that she loved seeing lights glow in the windows at night. Watching Belle chase squirrels around the yard. Hearing Nick's tuneless whistle when he was outside working. Witnessing the slow transformation that was turning a weary-looking house into a home.

Knowing that Nick and Beth belonged there.

Beth believed the house was an answer to prayer but was it possible it was the answer to hers, too?

Chapter Ten

"Okay, God. I'm listening."

Unfortunately, all Nick heard in response was silence. No still, small voice. Only the birds and the excited chatter of a squirrel warning its forest friends about the two intruders who'd crossed into their territory.

After the conversation with his mother, Nick needed to clear his head before he went to work. And since he couldn't hit the gym, he hit the trail along the river instead.

He still had a hard time believing that Beth had been asking God for a mother. But what was even more difficult to believe was that Beth thought Julia was the answer to her prayer! Julia lived in the country but dressed like a fashion model. She wasn't an animal lover. She froze whenever anyone invaded her personal space....

Except for last night.

Before he could prevent it, an image of Beth, nestled comfortably against Julia while they read the devotional book, popped up in Nick's mind. Immediately followed by another. The flash of longing he'd seen in Julia's eyes when he'd walked her home. It had taken all his self-control not to pull her into his arms but she'd severed the connection between them by walking away. She'd rejected his awkward invitation to dinner. In fact, other than a few rare smiles, she hadn't given any indication that she was interested in him. In fact, she made it a point to show him just the opposite.

Because she's afraid of what she's feeling. Just like you are.

Now Nick heard the still, small voice.

"I'm not afraid," Nick muttered. "I'm…content."

Content with memories of the brief but happy years of marriage to Liz, his high-school sweetheart. Content with the career he'd chosen. Content to pour his time and energy into their only child.

Wasn't that a good thing?

Nick couldn't help sounding a wee bit defensive when he'd directed the question at his mother.

"Contentment *is* a good thing. Protecting your heart from pain isn't," Claire had gently pointed out on the phone. "When I was about to turn down Robert's invitation to go out for dinner, a wise person said that I should be open to God's leading, even if it meant leaving my comfort zone."

Nick knew exactly who the wise person was that she'd referred to. But he hadn't expected his mother would turn his words around and use them on him.

The situation was completely different.

He'd have to have a talk with his daughter, that was all there was to it. Just because they'd moved next door to a young, single woman didn't mean that God had handpicked Julia Windham to be Beth's mother.

Or his wife.

He and Julia were neighbors. They'd barely formed a truce, let alone a friendship. Nick couldn't see anything else happening between him and Julia.

Even though you would like it to.

"A guy can only take so much rejection, Lord," Nick muttered. "I'd have to see a major breakthrough in Julia's attitude to even consider…" His voice trailed off.

Why was he considering anything?

Nick groaned. This was Beth's fault. And his mother's. For putting thoughts in his head that had no business being there.

Rather than wandering around like Moses in the desert, Nick decided it would be better to go to the office and focus on his work.

Speaking of wander. Nick frowned. He'd lost his walking buddy.

"Belle!" He called the dog's name and tilted his head to listen, expecting any moment to hear her crashing through the underbrush.

Nothing.

With a resigned sigh and a vow to bring a leash next time, Nick started toward the creek, knowing how much the dog loved to wade in the ice-cold water.

As he worked his way through the brush, he passed one of the many yellow No Trespassing signs that peppered the woods between the two properties.

The irony wasn't lost on him.

"That means you," he reminded himself sternly. "Julia Windham doesn't want anyone trespassing on her property. Or in her life."

Another trail opened up near a clearing by the river and as Nick rounded the corner, he heard Belle begin to bark. The frantic bark reserved for the impudent squirrels that dared to mock her from the safety of a branch above her head.

Nick broke into a jog as Belle continued to raise a ruckus loud enough to be heard in Clear Springs. Julia had already caught them on her porch. He didn't want her to catch them trespassing on her property, too.

"Belle! Come here, girl." Nick knew he was probably wasting his breath but if the dog stopped barking long enough to look at him, at least his eardrums would have a few precious seconds to recover.

Belle's head turned in his direction and there was a blessed moment of silence. Before she started up again.

Nick vaulted over a fallen log and almost fell flat on his face in his haste to get to the animal. "Do you know what the word *trespassing* means? It means that if Julia finds us here, we're going to be in big trouble."

Belle's frantic barking subsided to a high-pitched whine but she continued to dance around the trunk of the tree.

"When are you going to learn that you can't bark a squirrel out of a tree?" Nick peered up at the branches, expecting to see one of the fuzzy little critters grinning down at them.

What he didn't expect to see was…Julia.

He blinked, just to make sure she didn't vanish like some kind of forest sprite. No. Still there. And not looking at all happy to see him. Belle, on the other hand, gave him a smug, see-what-I-found grin.

"You're sitting in a tree." *Brilliant powers of observation. Maybe you should have been a detective instead of a veterinarian.*

"And you're trespassing."

Nick had hoped she wouldn't notice. But apparently he wasn't the only one who possessed brilliant powers of observation. "You weren't spying on me, were you?" The thought, however far-fetched, cheered him.

"No." Julia looked a little nonplussed by the suggestion. "Just thinking. *Alone.*"

Instead of taking the hint, Nick leaned against a tree and stuffed his hands in his pockets. "Great. Let me know when you're done."

She gaped at him. "You aren't going to wait for me."

"That's the plan."

"I climbed up here," Julia pointed out. "I can get back down again."

"Convince me."

"I've climbed this tree a hundred times. Look at the branches…it's like going up and down a ladder."

Nick studied the large gaps between the gnarled limbs of the oak. "You're right, I have seen ladders like this. In Beth's Dr. Seuss books."

Something in his expression must have convinced Julia that he wasn't going anywhere. She started climbing down.

By the time she reached the last branch, Nick was there, ready and waiting for that final four-foot drop. His hands closed around Julia's narrow waist as she swung down.

"Feel better?" Julia grumbled the moment her feet touched the ground.

"Yes." A lot better. That was the trouble. It suddenly occurred to Nick that he hadn't let go of her yet. It suddenly occurred to him that he didn't *want* to.

"Nick."

When Julia whispered his name, Nick couldn't have stopped himself from looking at her lips if his life had depended on it. He lowered his head, wondering if they were as sweet as he imagined.

Are. You. Insane?

Out of nowhere, the voice of reason drenched him like a bucket of cold water. Reminding him that if he crossed that line, she'd never speak to him again.

"I'm sorry…." Nick stopped, fascinated by the blush of color that stained Julia's cheeks. And the look of absolute disappointment on her face.

She pivoted away from him and started down the trail.

If Nick's knees hadn't turned to sponges, he would have gone after her. He looked down at Belle.

"Do you think that qualifies as a breakthrough in her attitude?"

The dog barked once in affirmation and Nick grinned.

"So do I."

Chapter Eleven

"Julia? I was hoping I'd catch you at home."

When, Julia wondered, was her heart going to stop ricocheting around in her chest whenever she heard Nick Delaney's voice?

Fortunately, it was easier to deal with him on the telephone than in person. On the phone she didn't have to shore up her defenses against an engaging smile and a pair of warm green eyes.

"I'm actually not at home right now. I'm at the grocery store."

"I'm afraid this is becoming a habit. Calling you in the middle of the day to ask for a favor." Nick's low laugh proved to be just as dangerous to Julia's peace of mind. It conjured up memories of the day before, when he'd caught her sitting in the tree.

She'd heard Belle barking and Nick whistling for her to come back. She'd hoped neither of them would find her. She hadn't anticipated the dog could boast a bit of bloodhound in its genes. Upon discovery, Julia had done her best to brazen her way through it and she'd nearly succeeded...

Until Nick had almost kissed her.

It was your imagination, she chided the mischievous voice in her head.

Mmm. So you must have imagined your disappointment, too?

This time, she ignored the pesky thought.

Nick had walked with her to the property line, but once they had gone their separate ways, all of Julia's old fears had crowded in. She wanted to believe. To trust. But what would happen if she lost everything again?

"What can I do for you?" She was relieved to discover that her voice was steadier than her shaking hands.

"I don't know if Beth mentioned that her birthday is today?"

"A few times." Julia smiled. More like half a dozen. "She seemed pretty excited, even though she got her gift early."

"Early?"

"Belle. I remember Beth saying that she was hoping to get a puppy this year."

"Yes, well…I found something else. Irma Robertson is taking Beth out for ice cream after school and I was wondering if I could stash the present in your barn. To surprise her when she gets home."

"I suppose so." Julia fought to keep her emotions grounded against the ridiculous surge of pleasure at being included in Nick's plan.

"I'm on my way home now. Do I need to wait for you? Irma promised she'd keep Beth busy until four."

Julia glanced at her watch. It was almost two o'clock. "I've got a few more errands to run but the barn isn't locked."

"One more thing." The husky timbre of Nick's voice sent shivers dancing up her arms. "What's your opinion of chocolate cake?"

"Chocolate cake is always good," Julia said cautiously.

"Good, because when I told Beth she could have some friends over to celebrate her birthday tonight, your name was the only one on the guest list."

"Really?" The word stumbled out before she could prevent it.

"Really." There was a smile in his voice. "If you don't have any plans."

None that compared to spending the evening with him and Beth.

"Should I bring something?"

"Just yourself. That's enough."

Julia hung up the phone, wishing it were true.

When had "just herself" ever been enough?

Nick heard the snap of a car door and strode out of the barn, relieved that Julia had arrived before Beth.

He could use some reinforcements. Now that the birthday gift had been delivered, he was having some doubts about the timing of his purchase. And those doubts had more to do with Julia's potential reaction to the gift than Beth's.

There was only one way to find out.

Nick stepped outside as Julia slid out of the driver's seat. Unaware of his presence, she tipped her face toward the sky and closed her eyes. Sunlight ignited threads of gold in her hair, and the simple design of the dress she wore emphasized slender curves.

The carefree gesture surprised him. He hoped it wasn't his imagination, but her attitude seemed to be softening. And she had accepted his invitation to celebrate Beth's birthday with them. That had to mean something.

"Did you need help carrying anything in?"

Julia started at the sound of his voice but couldn't quite conceal the flash of pleasure in her eyes. Nick hoped that meant something, too. "I didn't realize you were still here."

"Irma called me a few minutes ago and they're on their way back. Do you want to take a quick look before the unveiling?"

"Is Beth going to be as excited as you are?"

She was actually teasing him.

One step forward, Lord.

As they entered the barn, Julia stopped so abruptly that Nick almost bumped into her.

"That's a…"

"Horse." Nick strung the last word onto the sentence when her voice broke off. "Someone called the office and asked me to do an animal welfare check on some dogs at a place out in the country a few days ago. When I got there, I saw Star standing in a pen not much bigger than the kennel they kept their hounds in. The owner mentioned she had a one-way ticket to an auction this weekend."

Nick had been able to guess its fate from there. The faint outline of the animal's ribs was visible beneath the dirty sorrel coat. Clumps of burrs matted the mane and tail.

A horse like Star would have been easily overlooked as a potential riding horse, but Nick had taken one look at the sweet-faced mare, up to her fetlocks in mud and waste, and dug out his checkbook.

"You bought Beth a horse."

Something in Julia's flat tone sowed more doubt. "I know Star isn't much to look at, but I checked her over and there doesn't seem to be anything wrong with her that some TLC from a little girl won't cure. I promised Beth we'd get a horse if we found a house in the country. I didn't think it would happen this fast but I think she'll work out fine." The fact that he was rambling made Nick wonder who he was trying to convince.

"What are you going to do with her?"

"Tom said there's a riding club in the area that offers lessons for beginners—"

"I mean now," Julia interrupted curtly. "Tonight."

Nick had thought that was what she meant. "I was hoping you would let us board Star here for a few days until we can put up some fencing and a shelter of our own. I'd pay you, of course—"

"You want to keep her *here?*" Julia's voice thinned and cracked on the last word.

"Just for a few days. You won't even know she's here. Beth and I will take care of everything."

"Good. Because I'm not having anything to do with it."

Nick's eyes flew to Julia's face. Her skin was bleached of color, a stark contrast to eyes as dark as uncut amethysts. She whirled around, a slight hitch in her step as she stalked toward the door.

So much for one step forward.

Nick knew he'd just taken two giant steps back.

Julia was afraid of horses.

"Is she really mine?"

"Hey! You're choking me." Nick gasped as Beth wrapped her arms around his neck. "And yes, she's really yours."

Beth loosened her grip. "What's her name?"

"Star." Nick's throat tightened at the look of wonder on his daughter's face. "Happy birthday, sweetheart."

"She's beautiful. Did Julia see her yet?"

That was a definite yes. "She stopped in the barn for a few seconds."

Before she left him standing in the barn, an apology dying on his lips.

"Are we going to keep her here?"

"Not permanently." Nick quickly set Beth straight. "And it's up to you to do the work. Making sure she has fresh water. Feeding her. Grooming her."

"Work? That's going to be fun." Beth giggled when Star stretched her neck over the fence and the velvet lips nuzzled her palm. "When can I ride her?"

"Let's give her a few days to settle in to her new home first," Nick suggested. "Granna and Robert sent some gifts for you to open. Why don't we come back later to visit Star?"

"Sure." Beth gently stroked the mare's nose. "I'll get Julia."

"Ah, I don't think she's feeling very well today." Thanks to the bomb he'd dropped on her. "I'm not sure if she'll be coming over to have cake with us."

Disappointment stole the sparkle from Beth's eyes. "Maybe we could bring her a piece when we come back."

"Maybe." Nick would let Beth do the honors. He wasn't sure Julia would open the door if she saw him standing on the other side.

On the way back to the house, Nick silently berated himself for not telling Julia his plans in advance. It had seemed so logical at the time. She had a vacant barn and a fenced-in pasture. They had a horse that needed temporary lodging. A perfect match.

To make matters worse, as Beth had skipped ahead of him, Nick swore he'd heard her say, "That's two, God."

If it hadn't been for the conversation with his mother, he would have remained blissfully ignorant about what she'd meant.

And if Julia *was* part of God's plan, he'd definitely gotten in the way.

Chapter Twelve

The warm breeze stirring the kitchen curtains promised a beautiful day, and as Julia poured herself a cup of coffee she caught a glimpse of Nick and Beth coming up the driveway. Beth was practically skipping while her father followed at a more leisurely pace. Judging from the slouch of his broad shoulders and the tousled hair, Julia guessed that Beth had prodded him out of bed earlier than he would have liked on a Saturday morning.

Near the barn, Star nibbled spears of grass while waiting for her official breakfast—a flake from one of the bales of hay stacked in a corner of the barn—to be served.

Julia was relieved that the mare seemed to have a calm, friendly disposition in spite of the way she'd been treated. Most people would have dismissed the neglected mare outright. The fact that Nick hadn't made her respect him even more.

But it still didn't mean she wanted the horse living in her barn.

Don't get involved, Julia warned herself as she stepped away from the window before they spotted her. *The only thing you agreed to provide was temporary housing.*

She knew Nick hadn't understood her reaction when she'd seen Star in the barn. Julia hadn't quite understood it herself. The only thing she did know was that her heart hadn't been prepared for the avalanche of memories that crashed over her. Or what to do with them now that she could no longer shut them out.

After Nick and Beth had gone home, she'd picked up the phone to call Nick and tell him that she couldn't come over for Beth's birthday celebration.

But when it came down to dialing the number, she couldn't do it.

On the way over to the Delaneys', Julia had told herself that all she had to do was drop off the gift, but Beth's shining eyes when she'd opened the door had derailed her plan. She'd stayed.

She and Nick had maintained a polite distance throughout the evening but there'd been times she'd felt his searching gaze on her. Knowing he had an uncanny way of reading her thoughts, Julia hadn't been able to scrape up the courage to look at him.

She'd seen him raise a questioning eyebrow in her direction when Beth had opened her gift. Julia had mentioned that she worked out of her home but hadn't told Nick what she did. That was why she'd hoped Beth wouldn't notice the words *Wind River Farm Designs* embroidered on the label of her new riding jacket. But she had. And it had only added to the questions brewing in Nick's eyes.

Questions Julia didn't have answers for.

Fortunately, when it had come time for her to leave, Nick hadn't offered to walk her home.

Julia had been relieved…and disappointed.

It was those conflicted emotions that kept her inside now. Away from the man who caused them. She tackled several household projects instead. Her sink and shower were spotless. The floor mopped. She even organized her desk drawer.

Her curiosity finally got the better of her and she peeked out the window. She was surprised to see Nick and Beth standing on the opposite side of the fence from Star, watching the horse daintily finishing off her breakfast.

Something about the morose slump of Beth's shoulders set off warning bells in Julia's head. Without thinking, she pushed the door open and stepped outside to find out what was wrong.

"Good morning."

Nick turned around. In spite of the tension between them the day before, he didn't bother to hide his relief at her approach. "Good morning. Beautiful day, isn't it?" He didn't sound very convincing.

"Yes, it is." Julia's gaze moved from Nick to his daughter. "Hello, Beth. You're up bright and early this morning."

"Yeah." The girl managed a smile but Julia didn't miss the diamond-bright sheen of tears in her eyes before she looked away.

What had happened?

Julia propped her arms on the fence and did a brief but thorough assessment of the animal on the other side. Nothing appeared to be amiss.

"How is Star this morning?"

"Good." Beth's lackluster response didn't do anything to ease Julia's concern. Was it possible she wasn't happy with her new horse? In spite of the earlier vow she'd made not to get involved, Julia had to find out why Beth seemed so dejected.

She glanced at Nick, a question in her eyes, and his helpless shrug brought her to a decision. "I came out to tell you that I put on a fresh pot of coffee and there's a pitcher of lemonade in the fridge. It's getting warm out here so I thought maybe the two of you would like something to drink."

"That would be great." Nick didn't hesitate to take Julia up on the offer. "I'll give you a hand."

"Beth? What about you?" Julia asked.

In response to her question, she received a halfhearted shrug.

Julia waited until she and Nick were out of earshot. "What's the matter?"

Nick shook his head. "I'm not sure. Beth could hardly sleep last night, she was so excited. She woke me up at six-thirty raring to go, but when we got here, it was almost like she…shut down or something. She talked to Star and gave her a treat but that was it. I can't even convince Beth to brush her." Frustration leaked into Nick's voice but Julia sensed it was aimed at himself rather than his daughter.

"Is it possible that Beth is afraid of her?" she ventured.

"Afraid?" Nick repeated the word as if it hadn't crossed his mind. "No. She has an entire library of books about horses. How to groom them. How to take care of them. How to saddle and bridle them. Braid their manes and tails. Everything."

"But has she ever actually *done* those things?" Julia asked patiently.

Nick stepped ahead of her and held the door open. "Sure. The day camp she attended last summer offered trail rides for the girls."

Julia could guess what that experience had been like. To save time, the counselors would have had the animals all saddled and ready to go. Then the seasoned trail horses would fall in line, single file, down a path so familiar it would be like sleepwalking.

"No matter how much Beth loves horses, their size can still be intimidating to someone her age," Julia said carefully. "She doesn't know Star well enough to trust her yet. And vice versa. When it comes to horses, trust is a two-way street."

Nick blew out a sigh. "Any suggestions?"

Julia hesitated. She had plenty of suggestions—she just wasn't sure she could share them. Not without breaking her rule.

Are you trying to tell me something, God?

She silently raised the question with an equal blend of frustration and humor. She'd opened her heart to His leading the day before and already He was taking her to places she wasn't sure she was ready to go.

"Why don't you take a glass of lemonade to Beth? I'll be out in a few minutes."

Concern, and a touch of disappointment, skimmed through Nick's eyes but he nodded.

Julia sagged against the counter as the door shut softly behind him.

"I'm not sure I can do this, Lord," she whispered.

It was the second time her thoughts had instinctively turned toward God. The moment she whispered the words, Julia felt an immediate peace as a quiet voice seemed to echo through her soul.

I'll help you.

"Do you want to put Star's halter on and walk her around the yard?" Nick handed Beth a glass of lemonade and propped one booted foot against the fence rail.

"I don't know." The tears welled up again.

Nick was at a loss. "It's going to be difficult for you and Star to get acquainted with a fence between you," he pointed out gently.

"I know." Beth's miserable gaze strayed to Star, who lifted inquisitive ears in their direction.

"Is Star ready for her day at the spa?" A voice sang out. Familiar and yet...not.

Nick turned and saw Julia. It was, he decided, a good thing one of his feet was hooked over the fence rail or he might have fallen over.

The Julia striding up to them had traded in her pristine khaki slacks and cashmere sweater for a pair of figure-hugging jeans and a faded cotton T-shirt. Scuffed, knee-high riding boots replaced the expensive shoes she usually wore and a ball cap covered her tawny hair.

She looked...beautiful.

Beth's eyes widened at the transformation but she recovered more quickly than Nick. "Spa treatment?"

"Sure." Julia's engaging smile surfaced. "We'll give Star the Wind River Farm special. Bath. Shampoo. Pedicure. The whole works."

"Cool!" Beth dashed toward the barn but Nick caught up to Julia and snagged her elbow.

"You don't have to do this," he murmured. "I know that you're...you know."

Her expression closed. "I'm what?"

She was going to make him say it. "Afraid of horses."

"Afraid of horses."

"I saw your face yesterday. You looked like you were about to pass out. It may take a few days but I can make some phone calls and get someone to come out and show Beth what to do."

"I appreciate your concern, Nick, but I'll be fine."

Unconvinced, Nick searched her face, looking for the signs of fear he'd seen the day before. Instead he saw something that looked a lot like...laughter.

Chapter Thirteen

"What is this called?" Julia held up a metal tool for Beth's inspection.

"A hoof pick," she responded instantly.

"Right." Julia smiled in approval. Nick had been right. Beth did know a lot about caring for horses. All she needed was the confidence to apply that knowledge.

It helped that Star patiently accepted their efforts. As Julia suspected she would, the mare soaked up all the attention like a tilled garden during a summer shower. The espresso-brown eyes drifted shut in a state of absolute bliss as Julia took a shedding blade and scraped away what remained of the horse's shaggy winter coat. And she stood perfectly still while they undertook the painstaking process of removing the burrs from her mane and tail.

As the morning progressed, Beth turned out to be a willing pupil, eager to learn how to care for the horse herself.

"And what do you need to do when you're cleaning out the hooves?" Julia asked.

"Be careful not to hurt the frog."

"She has a frog in her foot?"

Julia started at the sound of Nick's voice. Not that she'd forgotten he was there. That proved to be impossible considering he hadn't been more than two or three feet away from her for most of the morning. Not surprisingly, he was as gentle and patient with Star as he was with his daughter.

Several times, Julia had felt his gaze settle on her but she'd been careful not to make eye contact. Too dangerous. She'd seen the questions in his eyes when she'd retrieved her old grooming bucket from the tack room, but fortunately they'd been so busy that he hadn't had the chance to voice any of them.

She still couldn't believe he'd thought she was afraid of horses.

Tell him.

Julia shook the thought away. She couldn't. Not yet. Maybe not ever.

Beth giggled. "The frog is part of the hoof, Dad."

"I think you'll have to lend me some of those books you have." Their eyes met over Beth's head and Nick winked at her. Julia felt the impact clear down to her toes.

Flustered, she knelt down, talking to Star in a reassuring voice as she ran her hand down one fetlock. The horse obediently picked up her foot.

"Good girl."

In response to Julia's praise, Star swung her head around and gently lipped Julia's hair.

"Hey, none of that now," she admonished.

Nick chuckled. "She must like the smell of jasmine."

He recognized the scent she wore? Julia's heart skipped a few beats. She flinched and Star's ears flattened at the sudden movement. Giving the horse's flank a quick, reassuring pat, she rose to her feet, praying that the muscles in her leg would cooperate. She didn't want to end up falling into Nick's arms.

Or did she?

"Beth—" Julia pushed the word out. "I've got some clean rags in the tack room. Could you get them? I think we're almost finished here." At least *she* was.

"Sure." Beth obeyed in a flash.

Julia immediately realized her mistake. Now she was alone with Nick.

Before he could ask the questions she'd seen lingering in his eyes all morning, Julia took hold of Star's halter and led her toward the stable door. "I'll turn her out for a while. She'll dry off faster in the sunlight."

Don't follow me.

Nick followed her.

"Here you go, girl. Enjoy the sunshine." Julia found it much easier to talk to the horse than to Nick. Apparently she hadn't changed as much as she'd thought! Why that surprised her, she didn't know. Her equine companions had always seemed more accepting than her human ones.

"Julia." The husky scrape of Nick's voice sent a shiver up her arms, put all the nerve endings in her body on red alert. "Thank you. I seem to be saying that a lot lately, don't I? But—"

Julia didn't wait for him to finish the sentence. She ducked past him and heard his huff of frustration. It made her move faster. "Beth must be having trouble finding the rags. I better help her."

There was no sign of the girl in the tack room but a knot formed in Julia's stomach when she saw another door standing wide open.

"I'm in here!"

There was no mistaking the excitement in Beth's voice. Which caused a second knot to form in Julia's stomach. She swallowed hard and entered the room, knowing exactly what she'd see inside.

Nick, who'd followed her—again—stopped short in the doorway.

"Who won all these trophies?" Beth pointed to the glass cases lining the walls.

Out of the corner of her eye, Julia saw the expression of disbelief on Nick's face. Somehow, that made it even more difficult to tell the truth. Not that she had a choice now.

"I did."

* * *

I did.

The words barely registered over the rushing sound in Nick's head. His emotions shifting to autopilot, he walked into the spacious room. With its leather furniture and paneled walls, it looked more like the kind of comfortable, well-appointed office a person would find in a home rather than a barn.

Beth pointed to a framed photograph above the sofa. "Is this your horse, Julia?"

Instead of denying it, as Nick expected her to, Julia gave a curt nod.

"What's her name?"

For a moment, Nick didn't think she would answer. And then, "Her registered name was A Midsummer Night's Dream but her barn name was Summer."

"Where is she now?"

"Beth?" Nick jumped into the conversation when he saw Julia pale. "It's time to clean up, remember?"

Beth took one look at Julia's stricken expression and realized her mistake. "Okay."

"How about giving Star a treat for being so patient during her bath?" Nick fished a carrot stick out of his pocket. "We'll be right there."

Beth slanted a worried look at Julia before she picked up the grain bucket and headed for the door.

Nick knew he should follow Beth and let Julia shut the door on her past, but he stepped closer to get a better view of the photograph instead.

Wearing a stylish tuxedo jacket, tan riding breeches and knee-high boots, Julia looked perfectly at ease astride an ebony horse. Her honey-blond hair framed features that were slightly younger. Softer. But it was the expression on Julia's face that Nick couldn't tear his gaze away from.

She looked happy. As if there wasn't anywhere she'd rather be.

All morning he'd been quietly amazed at the ease with which Julia handled both Star and his daughter. She'd known exactly what to do…as if she'd done it a thousand times. Now he knew why.

He shook his head. "No wonder you laughed at me for thinking you were afraid of horses."

"I didn't laugh."

Nick gave her a skeptical glance. "Maybe not on the outside."

A ghost of a smile touched her lips. "Like I told Beth—it was a long time ago." She shrugged. "A lifetime ago."

"But—"

"I used to ride. I don't anymore. End of story." Without a backward glance—at him or the reminders of her past—Julia slipped from the room.

Nick knew it wasn't the end of the story. But would she ever trust him enough to tell it?

Chapter Fourteen

"Julia! We're here!"

A familiar woof accompanied Beth's cheerful greeting.

Julia couldn't prevent a smile. Right on time.

Ever since the day she'd supervised Star's makeover, Julia now found herself part of the Delaneys' daily routine. After school, Beth would stop in to say hello before going to the barn to feed Star, deliver fresh water and muck out the stall.

The first time she'd shown up, Julia had been a little taken aback by the unannounced visit. Especially when Belle had scooted in and made herself at home on the rug in front of the sink while Beth entertained Julia with stories from her school day. By the third visit, Beth was comfortable enough to sneak a peek in the cookie jar on the counter.

Julia made sure she kept it filled.

She'd started to look forward to Beth's arrival. It was Nick's daily visit she tried to avoid. After supper, he would walk up to the barn to supervise Beth while she and Star took a sedate walk around the pasture. His laughter inevitably drew Julia to the window, where she would linger a moment to watch Beth, silently correcting her posture.

Back straight. Heels down. Hands low. Eyes forward.

Every time she was tempted to go outside and help Beth with her equitation, the man leaning against the fence stopped her.

Julia hadn't realized she was such a coward.

Only this time she wasn't avoiding Nick because she was haunted by the past. No, this time it was because she was afraid of the future.

"Look what I got at school today." Beth kicked off her boots on the rug inside the door and skidded into the kitchen, waving a bright green piece of paper.

Julia pointed to the cookie jar as she took the flyer. It was an advertisement for the Blue Ribbon Rendezvous, an annual horse show sponsored by a local riding club. She didn't need to read the rest to know what it would say.

Wind River Farm had once hosted the event.

"This is in two weeks."

"That's a lot of time. Isn't it?" Beth broke off a piece of cookie and fed it to Belle.

Julia looked over the list of events again. Some of them were geared for beginning riders but she couldn't help but compare Star to the horses Beth would be competing against.

"Are you sure you don't want to wait another month? There will be other shows this summer."

"Don't you think we're ready?" The silent appeal in Beth's eyes arrowed straight to Julia's heart. "Dad said that I should try because it's just for fun."

Just for fun. Julia wished she had heard those words at Beth's age. She eased her grip on the past. Tried to remember what was important.

"He's right. You and Star will do fine." Julia handed her back the flyer and was gifted with a bright smile. "What events do you want to enter?"

"All of them."

"I knew you were going to say that." Julia laughed and gave Beth an impulsive hug.

To her amazement, Beth clung to her. "Come on. Let's go."

"Go where?"

Beth snitched another cookie. "To the barn. We've got a lot of work to do before the show. I have no idea what I'm doing."

That, Julia thought, made two of them.

But she grabbed her boots, just the same.

Star balked at the first jump.

Julia hurried forward, bracing herself for the inevitable as Beth's feet came out of the irons and she pitched forward.

By the time she reached them, Beth had caught herself from catapulting over Star's head but the horse was still dancing in place, eyes rolling suspiciously at the unfamiliar object in her path.

"She's afraid of it," Beth said, shaken by the close call.

Julia put a soothing hand on Star's neck and the other on Beth's knee. "That's because you told her to be."

"Me?" The word came out in a squeak.

Julia smiled. "It's easy to think the horses are the ones that are brave and in charge because they're so big. But even though you're a team, Star has to trust that *you* are the one in charge. As you got closer to the jump, your posture changed. You tensed up and pulled back on the reins. Those were signals to Star that she should be afraid, too."

"I am kind of afraid of falling," Beth admitted in a small voice.

"You are going to fall."

Beth's eyes widened and Julia laughed. "It's inevitable, sweetheart. Everyone falls off at some point. The important thing is to get back on again."

Not that she'd taken her own advice.

"Okay." Beth eyed the jump apprehensively, not as inspired by the pep talk as Julia hoped she'd be.

"Go ahead and show Star there's nothing to be afraid of."

"Julia?"

"Yes?"

"Will you show her first?"

Nick walked over the rise just in time to see Julia and Star sail over a low jump set up in the pasture. The muscles under Star's glossy coat rippled as if an invisible current flowed beneath them.

Julia's delighted laugh danced in the background of Beth's exuberant applause.

His heart locked up at the sound and he raised his hand to wave as the horse swung around. But instead of returning to the gate, Julia turned Star toward the woods on the other side of the field and they cantered away.

"Isn't she amazing, Dad?" Beth raced up to him.

Amazing. Unpredictable. Irresistible. Beautiful.

Nick couldn't decide which description fit the best.

"I guess that's the reason she won all those trophies." He pulled Beth against him and gave her a fierce hug.

Beth giggled. "I was talking about Star, Dad, not Julia."

Oops. Busted. Nick felt his face grow warm. "She's amazing, too. Why did Julia come out to help you?"

"Because I asked her," Beth said simply.

Mmm. Maybe he should have tried that. Every evening when he walked over to Wind River Farm to watch Beth ride, Julia stayed in the house, holed up like a groundhog in January. He'd been wondering how to coax her out of hiding.

"I told Julia about the show. It's in two weeks but she thinks we'll be ready by then. But I couldn't get Star to go over the jump and Julia said it was because she knew I was afraid."

Which was why Julia had taken Star over the jump first.

I used to ride. I don't anymore. End of story.

Nick's throat tightened. He'd already come to the conclusion that he and Julia needed to talk. If he could ever get her alone.

While they waited for Julia to return, Beth shared more details about the show. It was Mother's Day weekend. Some of the girls from school were entering, too. She needed riding clothes. They would have to rent a trailer.

Nick's head was beginning to swim when Beth broke off mid-sentence, a frown settling between her brows. "Do you think they're okay? Where did they go?"

Nick's gaze drifted to the opening in the trees where Julia and Star had disappeared. More than twenty minutes had already gone by. "I'm sure they're fine. Why don't you go up to the house and finish your homework. I'll take care of Star when they get back."

"Okay." Fortunately, Beth was too exhausted to argue. "Tell Julia I'll see her tomorrow."

Another half hour went by and the sun had slipped behind the trees when Nick heard the soft, rhythmic thud of hoofbeats in the pasture. Relief poured through him. He'd been close to sending out a search party.

Nick took one look at Julia as she led Star into the barn and knew they hadn't taken a leisurely trail ride. Julia's hair was tousled and damp; her porcelain skin glowed with perspiration. She looked as if she'd been strapped to the back of a missile.

And loved every minute of it.

Neither of them spoke while Nick unfastened Star's bridle and Julia removed the saddle.

"Beth?" she finally asked.

"I sent her home to shower and finish her homework."

A flash of guilt crossed Julia's face. "I guess I lost track of the time."

"I didn't think time existed when a person traveled at the speed of light," Nick said mildly.

"I wasn't…" Julia stopped and caught her lower lip between her teeth, unable to deny it. "I wouldn't push Star too hard."

"I know that. I was teasing you."

A smile tipped Julia's lips and she gave Star's neck an affectionate pat before turning her out. Nick rolled his eyes. He was jealous of a horse. Pathetic.

Julia watched the horse trot into the pasture, one hand idly massaging her hip. "She's a good horse, Nick. Smart. Eager to please. She and Beth will make a good team."

"Beth told me about the show. It was nice of you to help her, even though, knowing my daughter, she probably didn't give you much of a choice."

"They'll do fine." Julia took a step toward the door. And then another.

It occurred to Nick that he'd gotten the very thing he'd been hoping for. A chance to talk with Julia alone.

"Good night." A third step.

One more and she'd be beyond his reach. Again. Nick decided to take a risk.

"Why did you give up something you love?"

Chapter Fifteen

Julia should have known Nick would wait for her to come back to the barn after her impulsive ride.

"I don't love it anymore."

"I don't believe you."

As if he didn't trust her not to make a break for it, Nick crossed the distance between them. Strong hands closed around her arms, but instead of making her feel trapped, his grip was warm. Comforting.

The gentle touch made her want to lean against his chest and draw from his strength. Even knowing that she didn't deserve it.

"Why did you give up riding? Did it have something to do with the accident?"

"You know about that?" Julia didn't know why it surprised her. Lucy or Irma Robertson had probably filled him in on all the grim details the minute he'd bought the house next door.

"I know you got hurt and I'm guessing it had something to do with horses. Did the doctors advise you not to ride? Is that it?"

"No, that isn't it." Julia twisted away from him. "I can ride. I just don't *want* to. Sometimes horses are a phase. Something a person outgrows."

"That may be true, but not for you. I saw the look on your face when you took Star over that jump tonight. You looked like a woman who was exactly where she wanted to be."

She refused to cry. Not in front of Nick. She'd managed to contain her tears for four years; she could hold them back a little longer.

"It's in the past."

"I don't think it is. I think it's something you carry with you every day." Nick reached up and brushed back the damp strands of hair from her cheek. "Tell me, Julia. *Trust* me."

Julia stared up at him.

Trust. It sounded so simple. Did Nick know he was asking the impossible?

"Whatever this is about, you don't have to go through it alone."

Julia wished that were true. But once Nick knew what she'd done—what she was capable of—she could stop dreaming about a future that included him and Beth.

Maybe that was reason enough to tell him.

She nodded, acutely aware of Nick's arm around her as he led her to the sofa in the trophy room.

A fitting place, Julia thought bitterly. Her emotions shut down when she looked at the photo of her and Summer on the wall. That girl was a stranger to her now. Acknowledging that made it easier to face the past. Made it seem as if she were a spectator rather than a participant.

"Summer and I were signed up for a riding competition in Kentucky one weekend, but a storm came through and the course turned to mud." Without closing her eyes Julia could feel the pelting rain. Hear the low keen of the wind. "Some of the riders withdrew because it was dangerous but Mom didn't want me to. There were people from the Olympic equestrian team there and we'd heard a rumor my name was being tossed around.

"Laine, one of the other competitors, tried to convince the judges to cancel the event. I knew my mother was counting on me to compete so I told them that completing the course depended on the skill of the rider more than the horse." The arrogance of the assertion still seared Julia's conscience. "I offered to prove the course was safe by riding any of the horses there. They took me up on it.

"I took Thor—Laine's horse—out. That was my idea, too." Julia eased her hand from Nick's comforting grip. "I wanted everyone to see she was being overly cautious. We cleared the first fence without a problem, but when Thor took the second one, he slipped and fell. On me. That's all I remember. I woke up in the ICU two days later. Then came three months of rehab, a broken engagement and the end of my riding career. Mom left the area because she couldn't face the scandal."

Or the daughter who'd caused it.

That was what hurt the most. For years, Julia had secretly questioned if her worth as a person was determined by how many trophies she won.

After the accident, she got her answer.

Julia's voice trailed off and when Nick reached for her hand again, she pulled away.

The self-recrimination in her tone, the empty look in her eyes, told Nick the rest of the story.

Why hadn't he put the clues together until now? The vacant stalls. Julia's reaction to Star. The walls she'd built around her heart. They all added up to one thing.

Guilt.

Nick recognized the symptoms. He'd dealt with those feelings after Liz died.

Julia blamed herself for what had happened that day. She hadn't forgiven herself for what had happened that day.

"Thor?" He had to ask. Had to know if that was part of it.

"They had to put him down. Laine loved that horse…like I loved Summer." She stared, unseeing, at the trophies on the wall. "I wanted to prove myself. Wanted to win. But instead I lost. Everything."

From her tone, it was clear Julia believed that she'd deserved it.

"What happened when you got home?" Nick remembered Lucy saying something about Tara Windham not coming home much after the accident.

"Mom took a job teaching riding lessons at a private school out of state. She sold Summer before I got home."

Another wound. And one, Nick guessed, that still hadn't healed. *Help me find the right words, Lord.*

"You have to forgive yourself. It's the only way you can put the past to rest and move forward." He paused, knowing that in this situation, he could speak from experience. "I blamed myself when my wife died. She'd asked me to give her a ride to the restaurant and I told Liz I didn't have time. If I would have gone five minutes out of my way, she might still be alive."

"That wasn't your fault. You didn't know what would happen."

"Neither did you." Nick saw the impact the words had on Julia. "Maybe that's the reason your mom left. She might still be battling guilt because she pushed you to enter the competition that day."

Julia immediately began to shake her head. Short, jerky little shakes that looked as if someone was asking questions she didn't want to answer. "No. Mom couldn't settle for anything less than the best. When I couldn't win anymore, she wanted to find someone who could."

"Or she couldn't stay on the farm and be reminded every day of what you'd lost," Nick said softly. "I know that guilt ate me up inside until I turned everything over to God. The whole angry, grieving mess inside of me. It made all the difference. He's the only one who can bring something good out of our messes. And Julia, that's what He wants to do for you. Trust Him."

Trust in the Lord.

The verse from Beth's devotional book.

Why wasn't she surprised? Lately, no matter what she was doing, it shimmered below the surface of her thoughts like background music.

Julia wanted to trust. Was trying to trust. But the changes God was making in her heart wouldn't change the consequences of the mistakes she'd made that day.

"Julia, I care about you. Beth cares about you." Nick's voice roughened with the intensity of his feelings. "I didn't think I'd feel this way again, but—"

"Wait." Julia stopped Nick before he went any further. "I told you that after the accident, my fiancé broke up with me."

"If the guy dumped you because you got hurt then you were better off without him."

Julia rose to her feet and wrapped her arms around her middle. She had to tell him everything, even knowing it would form a barrier between them. One that would prevent his feelings from becoming deeper.

Unfortunately, it was too late for her.

"My injuries caused hemorrhaging and they were severe enough that I ended up with scar tissue. The doctor warned me that it would be difficult—if not impossible—to get pregnant."

Julia saw Nick's eyes darken with denial as her words sank in.

She waited. One heartbeat of silence stretched into two.

It was the reaction she'd expected but she hadn't known how much it would hurt.

"It doesn't matter, Julia."

"It does to me." And it would to him. Maybe not right away. But when it happened, Julia knew her heart wouldn't hold up under the weight of Nick's regret. Or pity.

He was an amazing father. If he fell in love again…married again…he would want more children. And Beth would be a wonderful big sister.

Julia wouldn't take that away from them.

Chapter Sixteen

Nick stared out the window, hoping to catch a glimpse of Julia as she supervised Beth's evening riding lesson.

A glimpse had to be enough. For now.

He'd asked Julia for the truth and yet hadn't been prepared for its impact. In the split second of silence that followed her stunning disclosure, a chasm had opened up between them.

Julia had been honest with him but Nick hadn't been honest with himself or the depth of his feelings. Somewhere along the way, he had fallen in love with her. The realization had broadsided his heart. By the time he regained consciousness, Julia had misinterpreted his silence for doubt.

He'd spent several sleepless nights since then asking God what to do.

Nick was well acquainted with loss. He knew that Julia had to choose to turn her pain over to the only One who could set her free her from the burden she'd been carrying.

The front door slammed and Nick frowned as he stepped into the hall to see what the commotion was about.

"Daddy!" Beth skidded toward him.

Nick caught her in his arms, quickly checking knees and elbows for scrapes. Other than the tears streaming down his daughter's face, there didn't seem to be any visible signs of injury.

"What happened, Tig?"

"Is Julia mad at me? Did I do something wrong?"

Dread pooled in Nick's stomach. Although he and Julia hadn't spoken since the night in the barn, she had continued Beth's riding lessons in the evenings. No matter how she felt about him, Nick couldn't believe Julia would say or do anything to hurt Beth.

"I'm sure you didn't do anything wrong."

"But Julia said…" Beth gasped out the words. "She isn't coming to the show with us this weekend. She has other p-plans." She burrowed her face against his chest.

Nick gathered her closer and closed his eyes. He should have seen this coming. Julia had never said she would attend the show. Guilt had forced her into a self-imposed exile after the accident. It was one thing to help Beth prepare for the horse show behind the scenes, safe within the shelter of her own property. Another to expose herself to the stares and speculation of the same people who had once cheered for her from the stands.

"It's all right, Beth. I'll be there to help you."

"You don't understand," Beth wailed. "It's Mother's Day and all the riders are supposed to give a rose to their moms. If Julia isn't there, how am I supposed to give her one?"

Mother's Day roses.

He drew Beth to the couch in the living room and she melted against him.

"Julia isn't your mom, sweetheart."

Beth sniffled. "She would be if you got married."

The bones in Nick's body liquefied, making him glad he was sitting down. "It's not always that easy."

"But she likes you and you like her. I can tell." Fresh tears leaked out the corners of Beth's eyes. "But maybe she doesn't like me anymore."

"Julia likes you very much."

"Then why won't she come with us?"

Nick sent up a silent SOS. He didn't want to break a confidence, but Beth needed to know there was a reason for Julia's decision. "Do you remember how sad we were after Mom died?"

Beth nodded. "My heart hurt all the time."

Nick's throat tightened. "So did mine."

"Did Julia's mom…die?"

"No," Nick said swiftly. "But losing someone isn't the only thing that can make a person sad. Julia was hurt in a riding accident a few years ago and she had to give up a lot of the things she wanted to do."

"She doesn't look hurt."

"Not on the outside, but I think her heart still hurts, just like ours did. We have to give Julia time. Not push her to do things she isn't ready for yet, like the horse show." Or risking her heart again.

"You and I both know that God is the only One who can heal people on the inside. He helped us and we have to believe He'll help Julia, too." Nick took a deep breath but it didn't ease the weight pressing against his heart. "We have to pray. That's all we can do right now."

"Okay." Beth lifted her chin and Nick saw a determined gleam replace the sorrow in the velvet-brown eyes. "I'll pray."

"You're going to let me use that one?"

Julia smiled at the awestruck look on Beth's face. Her mother had sold most of the tack before she'd moved away, but for some reason had left the show saddle Julia had saved an entire year to buy.

"If you'd like. It needs a good cleaning, though." Julia set the saddle down on the blanket spread out in the grass.

"Are you kidding?" Beth's fingers traced the satin-smooth leather. "I love it."

"There's a matching bridle, too."

"Was it Summer's?"

"Yes." Julia wasn't surprised by the question. Summer had

become a favorite topic when she and Beth got together in the evenings to prepare for the upcoming show. What had come as a surprise was that Julia no longer minded talking about the horse she had once owned. She accepted it as another one of the amazing changes that had bloomed out of the conversations she'd been having with God recently.

Julia had always shied away from remembering the past, not realizing that by shutting out the painful memories, she'd closed out the good ones, as well.

Beth picked up a soft cloth and followed Julia's lead, rubbing oil into the leather. "Summer liked to jump, didn't she? I can tell because she looks happy in the pictures."

Julia wondered how many people would think it strange to hear a horse described as happy. She, on the other hand, understood perfectly. "It was her favorite."

"Star likes it, too. Dad said he's going to take a lot of pictures of us on Saturday."

Julia tensed.

As the day of the show drew closer, she'd wondered if Beth would try to convince her to change her mind about accompanying them.

"Dad and I are going out for ice cream tonight. Do you want to come?"

Julia blinked at the sudden change in topic, even as the thought of spending time with Nick caused her pulse to skip a beat. Ever since she'd told him about the accident, he had watched Beth's riding lessons from the fence that bordered the two properties.

Julia told herself—repeatedly—that she didn't mind. Nick had encouraged her to forgive herself for the mistakes she'd made, but it wouldn't change the high price she'd paid for them. A price she couldn't ask Nick to pay, too.

"I can't." Julia refused to let her gaze drift to the house across the pasture. "I have a lot of work to finish by Friday."

As the temperature rose and the number of horse shows increased, it was always a challenge this time of year to keep up with the orders that came in.

"Okay."

Okay? Julia felt a pinch of disappointment that Beth didn't seem, well, more disappointed.

A bell clanged and Belle's ears lifted at the sound. Apparently Nick had discovered that his daughter's ingenious device for calling the dog home worked well for eleven-year-old girls, too.

"I think Dad is ready to go." Beth bit her lip, obviously torn between going out for ice cream or staying to clean tack.

Julia hid a smile. Only a girl who loved horses would look so conflicted. "Go ahead. I'll finish up here."

"You're going to put everything back in the barn, right?"

Julia found the question a bit odd. "Right."

"Okay." Beth bent down and gave her a quick hug. "See you tomorrow."

Julia focused on the task, pretending not to notice when the Delaneys' car cruised past. Half an hour later, she anchored the saddle against one hip and carried it back to the barn. It was strange, but she'd noticed that the more she worked with Star, the better her leg felt.

The mare rattled the stall door when Julia entered the building.

"As if you don't get enough attention." Julia's laughter faded when she saw an enormous blue ribbon fashioned out of cardboard and bright blue tissue paper. But it was the words carefully printed at the top of the ribbon, spelled out in silver glitter, that stole her breath.

Best Neighbor.

The gesture was unexpected. Sweet. And so…Beth.

Julia knew it should have made her smile, but instead her vision blurred as she faced the truth.

She wanted to be more than a neighbor.

Chapter Seventeen

"What's the grin for?" Nick sat down on the swing next to Beth. "Did you get extra chocolate chips in your chocolate-chip ice cream?"

"Nope." She rolled her tongue around the base of the cone to catch a drip. "Just because."

Just because.

Nick's eyes narrowed.

Why didn't he believe her?

When Beth came home after her riding lesson, she told him that Julia had turned down her invitation to go out for ice cream. It was the cheerful tone in which she'd said it that struck Nick as odd. For someone who loved to spend time with Julia, he would have expected Beth's mood to reflect her disappointment.

He'd been more than a little disappointed himself.

"Because..." he prompted.

Beth's freckles began to glow.

"Okay." Nick crossed his arms. "What did you do?"

"Do?"

"Yes, do. The freckles don't lie. You've been up to something."

Beth became fascinated with a ribbon of clouds unfurling over the park.

"Now your ears are pink." Nick braced himself. "Out with it."

"I made Julia a blue ribbon that said *Best Neighbor* and I hung it in the barn where she would find it," Beth admitted in a rush.

"You do remember what I said—" Nick resisted the urge to add the words *two days ago* "—that we have to pray for Julia."

"I did pray."

"And let *God* work in her heart." He didn't resist the urge to emphasize the word *God*. "Remember?"

"I remember." Beth's forehead puckered. Nick sensed a "but" coming. "But—" He hid a smile. "Granna says that sometimes God wants us to be His hands on earth."

His mother did say that. Frequently. In fact, one of Claire Delaney Owens's favorite sayings was, "God likes to use our arms to hug people."

"She's right." Nick couldn't deny it.

"That's what I remembered when I prayed about Julia." Beth peeked up at him through a fringe of silky copper bangs. "I know that God is working on Julia's inside, but it doesn't mean we can't do something on her outside, does it?"

The question punched the air out of Nick's lungs.

Out of the mouths of babes. Or in this case, precocious eleven-year-old girls!

He'd decided that giving Julia time to work through the past was the best decision. Knew that grief and guilt could paralyze a person's faith. But now, looking back, Nick realized it had been his mother's patience, coupled with the simple, loving acts of kindness from fellow believers, that had helped him find his way out of the darkness after Liz died.

Nick hadn't wanted to get in God's way, but what if Beth was right? Julia had been alone for a long time. Maybe instead of space, she needed someone to care enough to trespass over her boundaries.

"So the blue ribbon you made was for Julia's…outside?" Nick guessed.

"She hasn't gotten one for a while. I thought she'd like it."

The sparkle in her eyes warned Nick she had something else up her little pink sleeve. "Let me guess. You have another idea."

Beth reached into her backpack and presented him with a bright pink notebook and a glitter-filled pen. "It's all in here."

Nick wasn't sure whether to feel proud or terrified by the fact that she had a written plan.

He thumbed open the cover and sucked in an astonished breath when he saw the next idea on her list. "Beth, I don't think this one is…possible."

"But that's the best one," Beth said serenely. "And I'm already working on it." She tapped the tip of the pen against number three to refocus his attention. "You can be in charge of this one."

Nick didn't feel as if he were in charge at all.

But on second thought, maybe that was a good thing.

"Julia?"

Julia heard the kitchen door rattle and glanced at her watch.

Four o'clock.

Where had the day gone?

She'd sat down at the sewing machine right after breakfast and worked straight through lunch. When Julia had agreed to fill the order, she hadn't anticipated her evenings being taken up with riding lessons and all the last-minute details that needed attention before a show.

"I'll be down in a few minutes."

"Okay." Beth sang out the word and Julia's spirits lifted.

Order or not, she didn't mind giving up an evening for Beth.

Julia flipped off the light on the sewing machine and straightened up her work space.

A loud thump rattled the walls.

"What's going on down there?" she called. "Is Belle rearranging the living-room furniture again?"

"No." A giggle followed. "Can I turn the radio on, Julia?"

"I suppose so."

Seconds later, a familiar country-and-western tune spilled out of the speakers, filling every nook and cranny in the house.

More thumps. Maybe Belle and Beth were practicing line dancing while they waited for her.

Hopefully they wouldn't expect her to join in, Julia thought as she pushed her tired limbs down the stairs and rounded the corner into the kitchen.

The transformed kitchen.

"Surprise!" Beth grinned as Julia struggled to take in the change in her surroundings.

A vibrant peacock-blue silk tablecloth had been thrown over the plain, beige linen one she'd put on that morning. Colorful bowls surrounded a trio of chunky candles. The breeze stirred a collection of paper lanterns strung from the light fixture.

"What is all this?"

"It's Chinese food." Beth grinned. "Dad makes it for special occasions."

Dad?

"We thought you might need a break from cooking."

Julia's breath stalled as Nick appeared in her line of vision. The fact they hadn't spoken for several days didn't lessen the impact of seeing him face-to-face.

"Yes. Are you surprised?" Beth tugged her toward the table.

"Yes." Surprised. Speechless. Shaken. Julia wasn't sure which one to choose.

"I'll sit here." Beth claimed one of the chairs and pointed to the opposite side of the table. "You can have that one."

Which put her right next to Nick. Close enough that if she moved a fraction of an inch, their shoulders would be touching. As it was, she could smell the tangy scent of his cologne.

"Would you like to give thanks or should I?" He looked at her, and unexpected heat scratched at the back of Julia's eyes.

"You can."

"We hold hands when we pray." Beth reached across the table.

Julia could only nod mutely as Nick's fingers wove through hers. She felt the warmth and strength of his hand. And didn't want to let go.

"Lord, we thank You for your many blessings. For this food. For friends and family. But most of all, for Your love for us."

"And that You answer our prayers," Beth added in a whisper.

Nick cleared his throat. "And that You answer our prayers."

"So…" Julia fumbled to unwrap the pair of chopsticks next to her plate. "What is the special occasion? The horse show tomorrow?"

"No." Beth's pigtails swung in time with the decisive shake of her head. "This."

Julia frowned. "This?"

"Uh-huh. *This,*" Beth repeated, as if no other explanation was necessary. "Right, Dad?"

"Right." Nick aimed a look at his daughter that Julia couldn't quite interpret. And then he looked at her—with a slow smile that she was suddenly *afraid* to interpret.

Nick took the dishes over to the sink and rinsed them off. From his vantage point at the window, he could see Beth towing Julia toward the barn, chattering all the way.

All afternoon, when he should have been considering what to do about the rubber ball that Sean O'Grady's Labrador retriever had swallowed, Nick was wondering if their plan would backfire.

Beth had mentioned that Julia was trying to finish a special order for a customer. Her idea—number three on the list—had been to take Julia out for pizza. Nick figured she would come up with a reason to decline the invitation. That left one option. If Julia wouldn't go to a restaurant, the restaurant would have to come to Julia.

Right up until the moment he'd been stringing paper lanterns from the chandelier, Nick resisted the urge to make a quick getaway. But all his fears had been put to rest when Julia saw the table set for three.

Dinner seemed like such a simple thing. But when was the last time someone had gone out of their way to make Julia feel special? Loved?

Thank You, Lord, that Beth saw what I didn't.

No wonder Jesus had encouraged His disciples to have the faith of a child.

He dried his hands off on the towel and stepped outside.

The trailer he'd rented to take Star to the show in the morning was parked next to the barn. Washed, waxed and ready to go the next morning.

Every night, Beth had prayed that Julia would come to the show, but so far Nick had seen no evidence that she was going to change her mind. It was a struggle. He knew he should prepare his daughter for the possibility that Julia wouldn't show up, but he didn't want to crush her simple but steadfast faith, either.

You're in control, Lord. Beth and I are doing what we can on the outside and we'll trust that You're working in Julia's heart.

Chapter Eighteen

"Don't look at me like that. I came here to think. There's nothing unusual about that."

But maybe, Julia thought when Belle barked at her—for the third time in less than a minute—there *was* something unusual about explaining herself to a dog. While perched on the branch of a tree. At seven o'clock in the morning.

What was wrong with this picture?

Julia glanced at her watch. Again. The first event would be starting in a little over an hour.

Belle barked again.

"Fine. You win." Julia began to climb down, remembering the day that Nick had discovered her in the tree.

The day he'd almost kissed her.

Julia groaned.

What was the point in running away if your troubled thoughts came along for the ride?

She'd gone for a walk along the river, hoping the peaceful surroundings would make her feel, well, peaceful. Instead, as the minutes ticked by, Julia's restlessness only increased.

"I'm nervous, Julia," Beth had confided while they finished

packing the last of the equipment the night before. "Will you pray for me?"

The question had scooped out a chunk of Julia's heart. "Of course I will. You and Star will do great. All you have to remember is to have fun."

Now Julia imagined the announcer taking his place in the booth. The nervous energy of the horses shifting in the stalls. The organized chaos of the riders as they prepared for the first event.

Beth was probably terrified.

Julia closed her eyes.

I know You're with Beth, Lord. Remind her of that. Help her not to be afraid....

I'm with you, too.

The thought cut a shimmering path through the center of Julia's prayer. Exposing her own doubts and fears. Revealing the truth. She wasn't afraid of the stares or the whispers behind her back. She was afraid to trust her feelings for Nick. Afraid to risk her heart again.

She hadn't believed him when he'd told her the past didn't matter. Hadn't believed that someone could care about her after the mistakes she'd made....

But if she could trust God to heal the past, couldn't she trust Him with her future, too?

I don't deserve it, Lord. Nick said You make beautiful things out of the messes we make. I want to believe that You've been looking out for me. Loving me.

The words tumbled through Julia's mind as she took a shortcut through the woods that came out near the mailboxes.

What greeted her was a large, hand-painted sign fastened to a tree at the end of Nick's driveway.

Second Chance Farm.

The crooked letters were rose-petal pink.

Julia laughed out loud. Lifted her face to the sky.

"I believe you," she said.

Now she had to tell Nick the same thing.

* * *

The rose ceremony.

Julia's feet turned to lead.

How could she have forgotten the Blue Ribbon Rendezvous tradition? During the lunch break, the riders would stop in front of the outdoor bleachers, dismount and present mothers with a long-stemmed rose. The mothers would then take their place on the horses while their daughters or sons led them around the ring.

You can do this, she told herself. *For Beth and Nick.*

"Bethany Delaney from Second Chance Farm."

Julia heard the announcement and paused, wondering if Nick would be the one accepting the flower.

Someone suddenly grabbed her hand and began to pull her through the crowd.

"Nick!" Julia tried to dig in her heels. "What are you doing?"

"Hurry up. Beth is waiting for you."

"Waiting for me? How did you know I'd be here?"

"Where else would you be?" Nick grinned. "Beth has been praying. And so have I."

Before Julia could react to that startling bit of news, Nick's hands framed her face and he kissed her.

The scattered applause brought her back to reality and they broke apart. Nick didn't look the least bit repentant.

"Go on." He nudged her forward. "It's your turn."

Her turn.

For the first time in a long time, Julia let herself believe it.

She slipped through the fence and several of the mothers moved aside to make room for her.

Julia's heart almost burst when she saw Beth and Star crossing the ring toward her.

Only it wasn't Star she was leading.

Julia's fingers covered her mouth as the coal-black mare lifted her ears and nickered softly.

Summer.

But how could it be? Tears leaked out of the corners of her eyes as Beth stopped in front of her and presented her with a long-stemmed rose.

In a daze, Julia put her foot in the saddle and swung her leg over Summer's back. By the time they exited the ring a few minutes later, she couldn't see a thing.

"Hey." Nick was there, reaching for her. "I hope these are happy tears."

"How did you… Where?" Julia stumbled over the words.

"It was all Beth's idea but we had some help from an inside source."

Through her tears, Julia saw a blurred shape step closer.

She blinked them away and saw a familiar face. *"Mom?"*

Tara Windham nodded a little uncertainly but smiled when her gaze slid to Beth. "I got a call from a junior detective last week, asking if I knew how to find Summer. And then Nick came on the line and explained that you'd tried to find her a long time ago." Her mother looked away. "After the accident, when you were in the hospital, you said you didn't want any reminders of what had happened. I thought Summer would be one of them. I wasn't trying to hurt you, Julia. I thought I was…helping. I thought Summer would be a constant reminder that you'd lost your dreams. Your passion."

Not lost, Julia thought. Buried beneath a layer of guilt. And it had taken Beth and Nick to help her find it again.

"I didn't think I deserved to own a horse," Julia whispered, laying her head against Summer's neck.

"What you didn't deserve was what happened that day." She was stunned to see her mother's eyes fill with tears. Was it possible Nick had been right when he'd suggested that her mother had been wrestling with her own guilt?

"Your mother contacted some people and traced Summer to a family in Tennessee," Nick explained. "They agreed to sell her after I explained the situation, but we had no idea how to get her here in time for the show."

"*You* brought her here?" Julia looked at her mother in amazement.

"I was told that, and I quote, 'time is of the essence.'" Tara winked at Beth, who grinned.

"Are you surprised?" Beth hopped back and forth from one foot to the other, unable to contain her excitement. "I wanted to tell you last night but Dad said it would be better if we surprised you today when I gave you the rose."

"But how did you know I'd be here?"

"I prayed that you would talk to God about it," Beth said simply.

Nick reached for her hand, as if he knew that she needed something to hold on to.

She'd listened to her heart. Listened to God. And He'd brought her here.

"I'm…" Julia choked on a laugh as Summer nudged her arm, as if seeking some attention of her own. "I still can't believe you found her. *Why* did you find her?"

Beth rolled her eyes, as if she couldn't believe Julia had to ask.

"Because we love you, silly."

Julia glanced at Nick, almost afraid to witness his response to Beth's announcement.

"She's right. As always." Nick pulled Julia into his arms. Whispered in her ear. "We love you, silly."

Epilogue

❧

"I can't see a thing!" Julia laughed, putting her fingers to the handkerchief Beth tied around her eyes.

"That's the point." Beth giggled.

"No peeking, either, or you'll ruin the surprise." Nick's hand rested on the small of her back as he guided her across the kitchen and out the door.

"Another one? I thought the camera was my anniversary gift." Nick had tucked it in the corner of the tray, beside a tiny bouquet of wild violets, when he'd served her breakfast in bed that morning.

It was hard to believe that a year ago she and Nick had exchanged their wedding vows under the apple tree at Second Chance Farm.

"That was from Dad," Beth said. "This one is from me and Grandma."

"Oh, oh." Julia grinned. "Then it has to be something pink."

"The bow is pink," Nick said under his breath. "Careful. Here's the step."

Her heart stirred at the protective note in his voice. "Are you worried I'll fall over?" she teased.

"You are a little...off balance."

She couldn't argue with him there. Being seven months pregnant did tend to change a woman's center of gravity.

"Stop!" Beth gave the command and Julia tugged off the blindfold.

It took a moment for her to realize there was another horse in the pasture. The hollow-faced gelding had a choppy mane and a short, broomstick tail but his halter sported a cotton candy–pink bow.

"Your mom dropped him off an hour ago. She's in the barn getting another stall ready."

Julia smiled. Tara had come back to Clear Springs for the wedding and surprised them all with her decision to stay. She'd claimed there was no point in the brick house standing empty after the Delaney family had unanimously voted to take up residence in the old house across the field, but Tara's bluster hadn't fooled anyone. Beth had completely won over her adopted grandmother. And since her return, Tara had become as guilty as the rest of them of rescuing animals and transplanting them to the farm.

"So what do think, Mrs. Delaney?" Nick murmured in her ear. "Is there room for one more?"

Julia looked up at him. "Always, Mr. Delaney. Always."

"Do you like him, Mom?" Beth asked eagerly. "I named him Ranger."

"Ranger is absolutely beautiful." Or he would be, Julia thought, with some love and attention.

She felt the warmth of Nick's arms around her and smiled.

It was good to know there was plenty of both at Second Chance Farm.

* * * * *

Dear Reader,

I finally realized my dream of living in the country six years ago—and I haven't regretted it for a moment. Like Nick and his daughter, Beth, lots of space meant lots of room for animals!

Writing this book was fun because it gave me an opportunity to relieve those "horse crazy" years with our daughters. It was definitely a bonding time—we had some of our best conversations while mucking out stalls!

Whether you are a mother or a daughter (or both!) my prayer is that somehow God touched your heart through the pages of this book.

Blessings,

Kathryn Springer

QUESTIONS FOR DISCUSSION

Dreaming of a Family

1. Dixie dreamed of a handsome man who rescued her son from a fallen tree. Later, the tree fell, and she met the man! God often spoke through dreams in biblical times, but does He ever speak to or guide us in that manner now?

2. Dixie felt great guilt because of her husband's death. Yet Dixie could not seem to break free of her guilt. Why do you think this was? What could she have done to lessen her guilt?

3. Psalms 126:5 says, "Those who sow in tears shall reap in joy." How does this relate to Joel's situation? To Dixie's? Have you experienced an instance in your life that proves this verse?

4. When she first realizes that Joel is blind, she treats him rather rudely. Why do you think this is? What would you have done in the same situation?

5. When Samuel hurts himself with the saw, Dixie saves her father's life by calling 911 and getting the paramedics to the house fast. How would you have reacted in such a situation? Are there ways to stay cool under pressure in order to save a loved one?

6. Though she was falling in love with Joel, Dixie still had deep feelings for her late husband. Have you or someone you know had to learn to let go of your late loved one and go on with your life? Did you have a hard time moving forward? Discuss.

1. What caused Julia to keep her distance from people?

2. Both Nick and Julia experienced the grief that came from losing something dear to them. How did it change the way they viewed God? How did that have an impact on the way they saw the future?

3. The simple but real faith that Nick and Beth live out begins to soften Julia's heart. Has anyone impacted your life in a similar way? What were the circumstances?

4. Guilt can prevent us from letting go of the past. How was this true in Julia's life? What changed her?

5. It was Beth's idea to show Julia how they felt about her. What are some ways you've shown love to a friend or family member?

6. Beth named their place Second Chance Farm. How was this significant? Was there a time in your life when you received a second chance? What was it?

Here's a sneak peek at
THE WEDDING GARDEN
by Linda Goodnight,
the second book in her new miniseries
REDEMPTION RIVER,
available in May 2010 from Love Inspired.

One step into the living room and she froze again, pan aloft.

A hulking shape stood in shadow just inside the French doors leading out to the garden veranda. This was not Popbottle Jones. This was a big, bulky, dangerous-looking man. She raised the pan higher.

"What do you want?"

"Annie?" He stepped into the light.

All the blood drained from Annie's face. Her mouth went dry as saltines. "Sloan Hawkins?"

The man removed a pair of silver aviator sunglasses and hung them on the neck of his black rock-and-roll T-shirt. He'd rolled the sleeves up, baring muscular biceps. A pair of eyes too blue to define narrowed, looking her over as though he were a wolf and she a bunny rabbit.

Annie suppressed an annoying shiver.

It was Sloan, all right, though older and with more muscle. His nearly black hair was shorter now—no more bad-boy curl over the forehead—but bad boy screamed off him in waves just the same. He was devastatingly handsome, in a tough, rugged, manly kind of way. The years had been kind to Sloan Hawkins.

She really wanted to hate him, but she'd already wasted too much emotion on this outlaw. With God's help she'd learned to forgive. But she wasn't about to forget.

Will Sloan and Annie's faith be strong enough
to see them through the pain of the past and allow
them to open their hearts to a possible future?
Find out in THE WEDDING GARDEN
by Linda Goodnight,
available May 2010 from Love Inspired.

Former bad boy Sloan Hawkins is back in
Redemption, Oklahoma, to help keep his aunt's
cherished garden thriving and to reconnect with the
girl he left behind, Annie Markham. But when he
discovers his secret child—and that single mother
Annie never stopped loving him—he's determined
that a wedding will take place in the garden
nurtured by faith and love.

Where healing flows...

Look for

The Wedding Garden
by Linda Goodnight

*Available May 2010
wherever you buy books.*